MY FAMILY AND·OTHER ROMANS

MARIE BASTING

Chicken House

2 PALMER STREET, FROME,
SOMERSET BA11 1DS

Text © Marie Basting 2023
Illustrations © Flavia Sorrentino 2023

First published in Great Britain in 2023
Chicken House
2 Palmer Street
Frome, Somerset BA11 1DS
United Kingdom
www.chickenhousebooks.com

Chicken House/Scholastic Ireland, 89E Lagan Road, Dublin Industrial Estate,
Glasnevin, Dublin D11 HP5F, Republic of Ireland

Cover design by Steve Wells
Cover and interior illustrations by Flavia Sorrentino
Typeset by Dorchester Typesetting Group Ltd
Printed and bound in Great Britain by CPI Group (UK) Ltd, Croydon CR0 4YY

1 3 5 7 9 10 8 6 4 2

British Library Cataloguing in Publication data available.

PB ISBN 978-1-911490-95-1
eISBN 978-1-915026-61-3

For my own extraordinary parents,
Jim Lad and Joan Girl xx

Also by Marie Basting

Princess BMX

CHAPTER 1

ROME PLAY

'Come on, Livi! You know the drill!' called Dad from the far end of the garden.

'One potato.

Two potato.

Three potato.

Fire!'

A perfect hit. The arrow glanced off the brass

door knocker and landed next door in Mrs Burden's hollyhocks. Sighing, I pushed the Roman gladiator figures out of the way and opened my bedroom window.

'Seriously, Dad, why can't you just use the door-bell like everyone else?'

'Where's the fun in that?' He grinned, **centurion** cape flapping in the wind. 'Come, daughter, Rome Play awaits.'

Dad had been wearing a cape and tunic for nearly a month now. He said he wanted to get to know his inner Roman better. Still, it was better than his mythical being phase, I suppose. Trust me, being woken up by a cyclops on a dark winter morning is not good.

Welcome to my world! A world of foam weapons, muddy fields and fantastical adventures. A world where you can be a centurion, cyclops or sorceress for the day and still go the chippy for your tea. The world of **Live-Action Role-Play – LARP**. It's part acting, part dressing up and one hundred per cent awesome!

I'm Silvia, by the way – Silvia Fortuna Juno De Luca. It's a bit of a mouthful, isn't it? The sort of name you'd expect to belong to an Italian celebrity rather than a twelve-year-old who needs braces. But this is what happens when your dad is obsessed with Ancient Rome – so obsessed, we live practically on top of **Hadrian's Wall**, in a tiny village called Once Brewed. He had a dream, you see: to set up a mega role-play event dedicated to all things Rome. There's been a bit of a delay, what with me coming along and my mum doing a disappearing act, but finally his dream is about to come true. Rome Play!

Picture it as a sort of festival. Only, instead of chilling and listening to music, people pretend they're from the Roman Empire and hit each other with fake weapons. Honestly, it's going to be brill. Better than brill—

'Come on, Livi!' Dad unclipped his keys from the plaited leather lanyard around his neck. 'Kenzo is waiting for the paint I just picked up!' He turned towards the beat-up truck, pausing to breathe in the view of the sparse hillside where the late afternoon sun cast a golden glow over Hadrian's Wall.

Pulling the window shut, I legged it downstairs, slamming the door behind me.

'There she is!' said Dad as I shoved his sorcerer cloak off the seat and climbed into the truck beside him. 'My favourite daughter.'

'Dad, I'm your only daughter.'

'Not in Rome, you're not. I have seven. And you're still my favourite.'

I rolled my eyes – he was taking this whole in-character thing too far – but I couldn't help smiling. He was just so excited.

'Two more sleeps, Livi. Two more sleeps. I can't believe it's finally happening!'

'I know!' I returned his high five. 'You did it, Dad. You did it.'

Gravel scrunching, Dad pulled off, pausing where the drive met the road to tie his shoulder-length hair back in a ponytail with one of my old scrunchies. It wasn't very Roman.

'I thought you were going to get you hair cut like Julius Caesar.'

Dad shrugged and turned up the stereo. 'What, and lose the source of my great powers? Never!'

I laughed. I knew Dad wouldn't be able to bring himself to cut his hair. Not after those women told him he looked like Aragorn from *Lord of the Rings*. You see, it's not just fantasy Roman worlds Dad likes to escape to: Middle-earth, Camelot or Fantasia, you name it and the De Lucas will see you there. It's what we do – leave our problems behind and escape to somewhere better. A world where shattered dreams, forgotten promises and absent mums don't matter.

CHAPTER 2

DOOMED!

It didn't take long to get to the Rome Play site. Just long enough for me and Dad to belt out a banging rendition of 'Smells Like Teen Spirit' by Nirvana. Nirvana were this ancient rock band Dad got me into. Him and his mates are obsessed with them. They are a pretty obsessive bunch, the LARP lot, although from what I could see, nobody else at the site that day had felt the need to channel their inner Roman and dress up. It was all overalls and paint-splattered jeans.

Turning off the farm track that led up to the Roman fort of Housesteads from the visitor centre, we continued across the steep, rutted field to where the Rome Play village was being constructed at the top of the hill.

My heart sank like an orc in lead boots. It was nowhere near ready.

The huge canvas marquee, which was supposed to be camp HQ, was still being assembled, and most of the plywood buildings weren't even painted yet – Hadrian's ancient wall, snaking through the fields behind them, highlighting just how fake they were.

'We are a bit behind schedule,' Dad said, climbing out of the truck. 'I decided to fork out and get the hire company to erect the **contubernium** tents, but it's going to be tight with the triumphal arch. Although, our man Kenzo here promises me it will be here tonight.'

'Have faith!' said Kenzo, making his way over to us and high-fiving Dad. 'It's all in hand.'

The missing arch had been stressing Dad out for weeks after it was seized by customs in Calais. A replica of the Arch of Constantine, Kenzo had built it out of polystyrene for a TV show he was working on in Italy. He said it was going to take the site to a whole new level. Let's hope so, because right now Rome Play looked like it had been put together by our Year 7 design tech class.

Kenzo is Dad's best friend, by the way. He gets to go to all sorts of cool places for his special effects job. Can you believe he turned down the chance to work on the big Harry Styles concert because it clashed with Rome Play? It's the most mahoosive thing to happen round here since the Romans! But that's Kenzo for you. He's always been there for us – even if it was sometimes from a distance. And, yes, I know, bad timing or what with the Harry gig. But Dad was insisting everything would be golden.

'So, what do you think, Livi?' Kenzo said, holding out his fist for me to bump. 'Bit more basic than I'd have liked, what with the limited budget, but it will feel different when there are loads of people wandering around in costume.'

I put my hands on my hips and studied the plywood **forum**, trying to imagine what it would be like with loads of LARPers milling about in Roman gear. Kenzo was right. Most of the LARPs I'd been to had sets far more basic than this. It was the players and their imaginations that brought the world to life. And it was the players and their imaginations that would bring Rome Play to life too.

'It's going to be great,' I said. 'Amazing.'

And standing there, watching the volunteers buzzing about, I kind of meant it. There was already an energy about the place. The crew members singing as they unloaded gear from the back of Dad's truck; Kenzo's set design students sawing and hammering; and the little kids running around with wood-effect swords while their parents called out for them to be careful, all coming together to bring the place to life.

'How many tickets have you sold, Dad?'

'Oh, don't be worrying about stuff like that, Livi.' Dad flashed me his best smile. It's very Hollywood for a bloke from Runcorn, and seems to get him off the hook with most people. But it wasn't going to work on me. I followed him and Kenzo towards the mock tavern where a couple of teenagers I recognized from sword school were struggling to manoeuvre a giant table made of rough planks through the door.

'Just tell me, Dad. How many tickets—'

'Chill, Livi.' He patted one of the teens on the shoulder and gripped the edge of the table, Kenzo shuffling into position next to the other kid. 'I think most people will pay on the gate. You know how it is once word gets out.'

I chewed my nails, waiting for Dad and Kenzo to re-emerge from the tavern. We opened in two days. The word should have been out months ago.

'Just wait to see what I have planned for the pre-party,' Dad continued. 'People will be talking about it for years to come.'

Maybe they would. Dad did know how to throw a good party, but how was that going to help ticket sales? It would be too late by then . . . if it wasn't already.

'Maybe it wouldn't hurt to do a bit of last-minute publicity though, hey, Dad.'

'That's what I keep telling him.' Kenzo picked up one of the paint cans, stacked outside the tavern, and prised the lid off with a screwdriver. 'There are tons of press up here for the Harry Styles concert. Did I mention it's going to be the biggest drone light show ever?'

'Only like a million times.' Dad looked out across the valley towards the special stadium that had been built for the gig. His smile faded. 'Look, I'm sorry you missed out—'

'Don't be sorry,' said Kenzo. 'Just stop messing about and do the PR.'

I folded my arms, nodding in agreement. 'We need to sell more tickets.'

'Chill, the pair of you.' Dad put his hands on his hips. 'I'll have you know I'm a publicity guru. My

Facebook post had four likes this morning.'

'Ooh, check you out, Mr Influencer. I told you, Ben, nobody does Facebook any more.'

Kenzo handed me the tin of paint and nodded at the wooden facade opposite – a Roman-style shop complete with shutters and open-fronted serving counter. 'As for you, Livi, time to earn your keep. Can you give the shutters another coat of paint while I take your dad down to the main campsite? I'm afraid we have a bit of a portaloo situation in crew HQ.'

Dad screwed up his nose. 'And the toilet terror begins.'

'OK,' I said. 'But then we need to talk about the ticket sales.'

'The gate, Livi,' said Dad. 'People will pay on the gate.'

I rolled my eyes.

'Trust me, Livi. I have a few surprises in store that will get the whole LARP community talking. You are in for a treat!'

'But Dad, listen—'

'He'll soon listen when I stick his head down a portaloo,' said Kenzo.

'Yeah, right.' Dad grabbed hold of Kenzo and put him in a headlock. 'You and whose armies?'

Kenzo retaliated by hooking his foot around Dad's calf and pulling his leg from under him. They toppled to the ground in a heap where they rolled around play-fighting like a pair of five-year-olds, Dad flashing his Incredible Hulk undies.

Seriously, we were doomed.

CHAPTER 3

THE GREAT BATTLE
OF THE ORC

My shoulders were aching by the time Dad and Kenzo returned but I didn't mind. The shop looked so much better with the bright-green shutters. The hire company had started to erect the contubernium tents too. They were just like the pitched-roof leather tents the Romans used for their marching military camps, only smaller and without the fleas and mosquitoes. Well, at least I hoped they were without the fleas and mosquitoes. I also hoped people would actually want to hire them. Otherwise Brokeville here we come.

Not that Dad seemed overly worried about the ticket sales right now. His smile was nearly as broad as his shoulders.

'Nice job, Livi,' he said, tapping me playfully on the arm with his replica Roman sword. 'How about a bit of battle training as a reward? Chitra asked me to amuse the kids while she makes some final touches to the briefing sheets we've done for the crew.'

Chitra wrote the Rome Play script with Dad. Kenzo reckons they have a crush on each other. I hope not, because Chitra's twins are the worst whingers ever. Plus, Dad liking someone? I mean, ick!

'No sword. And anyway, we need to get back so you can start on the PR.'

'Oh, come on. I'm sure Kenzo has a spare you

can borrow. He never goes anywhere without a healthy supply of weapons.'

'Never,' said Kenzo, opening his transit van and throwing me a replica sword. He picked up his kitbag. 'To the fort.'

I glanced over to the elevated ruins where some of the little kids were playing soldiers. The crumbling stone walls were little more than waist-high but most of the foundations were still intact, and if you really used your imagination, it wasn't hard to picture what life at the fort would have been like 2,000 years ago when the Romans ruled Britannia. Shutting out Dad's battle cries, I let the images form: red-caped **legionaries** practising their drills on the slopes of Whin Sill, hopeful traders calling at the bustling barracks, and **auxiliaries** sharing news from home while queuing for the open-plan toilets!

'Come on, Livi.'

It was tempting. I mean, it's not every day you have the chance to spar in a Roman fort. I waved the fibreglass and foam sword, testing the weight.

It felt good.

It always felt good to spar and forget everything else.

Poking Dad with the sword, I legged it towards the fort!

'Non ducor, sed duco!' *I am not led, I lead!*

'Is that so?' Dad was hot on my heels. 'We'll see about that.'

Climbing up on to what was left of the gate tower, I breathed in the view and felt the tension in my shoulders lift. Dad was right. With the Roman wall snaking behind us and the rugged farmland stretching for miles ahead, this really was the perfect place to hold a Rome-themed LARP.

'OK, Livi.' An impatient Dad nudged me with his sword. 'Let's see what you've got.' He bounced playfully on his toes before edging backwards across the grass towards the sunken latrines where Kenzo was standing on the low wall with little Ari and Avi, Chitra's kids. The overgrown foundations uneven beneath my feet, I prepared to strike.

'Oh no you don't!' Dad jumped up on to the wall. 'You'll have to be quicker than that!'

I followed. Taking my chance as Dad stumbled on the uneven surface, I lunged at him with my sword. The dull thud of our weapons echoed around the fort.

'Come on, lads,' said Kenzo, nudging Ari. 'Let's spice this up.' He took his kitbag off his shoulder and rummaged inside, emerging with an orc mask which he pulled over his head and stretched into position. 'Charge!' he said, reaching for Ari's hand.

'No!' Ari folded his arms. 'No orcs in Ancient Rome!'

He kind of had a point – I'd read every book in Dad's classics collection and not once had an orc put in an appearance.

'It's just a game,' said Kenzo, thumping his chest and letting out a weird roar that I guess was supposed to sound like an orc. 'Come on, let's take them down!'

'Mask off,' cried Avi. 'No orcs allowed!'

Crimson-faced, fists curled into tight balls, he kicked Kenzo in the shin and flopped to the ground in an angry screaming heap.

'Off!' screeched Ari, showing his support for his brother. 'Take it off!'

'Now, boys,' Dad said, crouching down beside them, 'what are we going to do about this orc situation? They've been running wild throughout the empire. And I hear there is a reward for the brave soul who rids the land of them.'

'A reward?' The fire in Avi's cheeks dulled.

Ari, however, was not so impressed. He gave Dad a look even more blood-curdling than his screams. 'There were no orcs in Ancient Rome!'

'True,' agreed Dad. 'But there were monsters. Monsters that I believe could have evolved over the centuries into orcs.'

Ari hit himself in the head with his sword.

'Careful now, little dude. You'll need all your wits about you to help me defeat these foul creatures. I hear whoever slays the first orc gets a bag of chips and an ice cream sundae.'

'With sprinkles?' asked Avi.

'Of course, your efforts will be rewarded handsomely.'

Avi shrugged and looked at Ari, who wiped the snot from his face with the back of his hand and nodded.

'So, we have a deal then!' Dad clapped his hands together. 'Livi, if you wouldn't mind.' He pointed towards Kenzo's duffel bag, where a second mask lay on the ground. It looked like I was joining the orc gang too.

Dad waited while I slipped on the mask and jumped down from the wall.

'Charge!' he called, chasing me and Kenzo into the fort, the twins following close behind, tantrums forgotten. 'Nulla clementia! No mercy!'

Brilliant work, Mr De Luca! You've done it again!

It was Dad's gift, you see. Bringing people together, finding a way to compromise and keep everybody happy. Face raised towards the infinite sky, I beat my chest and let out an enthusiastic orc roar, allowing myself to escape into the game. Everything was going to be fine. Dad would make sure it was. Just like he always did.

CHAPTER 4

PART OF SOMETHING

Me and Dad were still laughing about the Great Battle of the Orc when we pulled on to the drive at home. Epic or what! It had turned into this mega fight with most of the crew setting down their tools and joining in. Nobody really knew what side they were on or what the deal was with the orcs, but none of that mattered. As Dad always says, LARP isn't about the winning, it's about the battle. Being part of something. Something special.

Slamming the truck door behind him, Dad glanced over to the paddock where the archery target had fallen over in the wind. 'Hey, how about a little shoot-out before tea?'

'I thought you were going to sort that publicity stuff. Isn't that why we didn't go for chips and ice cream with the others?'

'Come on, Livi.' Dad glanced over at the shiny new van parked up behind Mr Burden's Harley Davidson mobility scooter. 'Just a couple of rounds and I'll be right on it. I promise.'

I shook my head. I love archery – it's the one thing I'm any good at – but Dad needed to crack on.

'Winner gets to choose what we have for tea for a week.'

'A week?'

Dad smiled coyly – he knew I couldn't resist a challenge like that.

'OK,' I said, wrapping Dad's sorcerer cloak around my shoulders to protect me from the early-evening chill. 'But then you do the PR.'

'Deal! I'll sort the target; you get the bow!'

'Brill!' I turned on my heel.

But then I saw him.

Rory Smartwart – climbing out of the van on the Burdens' drive.

'Loser,' he mouthed, holding up his mobile and snapping a photo of me and Dad. He made an L shape with his finger and smirked.

My heartbeat quickened. The school bus was going to be hell tomorrow.

'What you looking at, son?' Mr Smartwart glanced over the low stone wall, brow furrowing, eyes scrunched like he was struggling to believe what he was seeing. He didn't say anything, but I knew what he was thinking.

Anger rose in my chest. But I wasn't mad at Rory. I was angry at myself.

Furious I wasn't strong enough to ignore what the Smartwarts might think and carry on over to the archery target.

Appalled that just the thought of what Rory might say to the kids in school was enough to send me scurrying towards the cottage.

Ashamed of how readily I abandoned Dad and legged it inside, wishing I had a dad that did DIY and watched the footie instead of running around in fancy dress.

CHAPTER 5

TROLL GIRL

Before Rory Smartwart started at our school, none of the other kids were bothered about the LARP thing. Some of them even thought it was cool. While they spent their weekends visiting grandparents or going to the supermarket, I went to sword school and camped out with orcs and wizards. They were curious. Coming to our house for tea was its own adventure. With Dad's endless games, the lack of rules, and nobody telling you off for traipsing mud into the house, it was every kid's dream.

But we weren't little kids any more, as Rory loved to remind everyone. And dressing up and role play was *seriously* uncool.

Which made me a *serious* loser.

A loser with a capital L, according to Rory.

His name-calling didn't bother me too much at first. He was clearly a gnat brain and I still had Mina and Jackson. But now it looked like they were avoiding me too. Last time I'd invited them over, they'd said they had dance practice. Which is what they'd said the time before too. And the time before that. Who was I kidding? They were never coming around to finish that D&D game.

'Livi!' Dad knocked again on my bedroom door. 'Livi, are you OK?'

'Go away, Dad!'

I felt bad as soon as I said it. But I just couldn't deal with one of his cheery pep talks right now.

'Just ignore them, Livi, you're stronger than that. When they realize you're not rising, they'll get bored and move on.' Thanks for that Dad, but that's kind of the problem. Everyone has moved on and left me behind.

'Come on now, love. How about a nice hot chocolate?'

According to Dad, hot chocolate is the solution to everything.

Stood in dog poo in your new trainers? Hot chocolate!

Nobody wants to sit next to you on the school bus? Hot chocolate!

Wondering why your mum abandoned you when you were a baby? Hot chocolate!

Hot chocolate! Hot chocolate! Hot chocolate!

I buried my face in the lumpy pillow, trying to shut it all out. Rome Play was going to make everything a zillion times worse.

Behind the door, Dad let out a deep sigh. 'OK,' he said. 'I'll leave you to it. But if you do decide you want some company, I was just about to stick a pizza in the oven and watch a film. *Ben-Hur* maybe to get us in the mood?'

I pulled my hood up. I just wanted it to all go away. 'I've got a headache.'

'That's a shame. I thought we could light a fire and toast some marshmallows too. I don't know about you, but I think it's been far too long since we had a proper cuddle night.'

Cuddle nights are what *normal* people call movie nights. At one time, we used to bring all my teddies downstairs and snuggle up with them on the sofa under the duvet. Each and every one of them would get a marshmallow and a kiss on the head off Dad. I'm too old for all that now, but I still like it when we snuggle up on the sofa together.

But not tonight.

I couldn't take any more Rome Play talk.

'Come on, love. It will be fun to hang out together. Maybe we can live a little dangerously and have some dough balls with our pizza or something. You know, **LARPe Diem** and all that.'

'Why does everything have to be about LARP?'

The door edged open.

'Go away, Dad!'

'Livi, what's wrong, love?'

'Nothing. I'm just not a little kid any more.'

'What! You're growing up? Stop it right now!'

Blood thundered in my ears. 'Do you know how much people laugh at us?'

I know, I know – I'm a terrible person being mean to Dad like that. But everything just seemed to catch up with me that night. Believe me, after what happened next, I'd have done anything to take those words back. Anything. But I'm getting ahead of myself...

'I think people are far too busy with their own lives to worry about us.' Dad was smiling but the wobble in his voice gave him away. 'Look, I'm going to go and stick that pizza on. Maybe when you've calmed down we can have a proper chat. Because I'm here for you, Livi. I'm always here.'

CHAPTER 6

TV TROUBLES

What was that? I sat up suddenly, the illustrated retelling of the *Aeneid* I'd been reading thumping to the floor. Loud and shrill, the continuous chirping sounded like a smoke alarm. Oh my Roman deity, it *was* a smoke alarm! The smell of burning hitting me like orc breath, I threw the bedroom door open and legged it downstairs.

'Dad?'

The TV screen flickered, turning the smoke tendrils drifting from the kitchen amber.

'Dad, where are you?'

Nothing. Except for the *chirp chirp chirp* of the smoke alarm.

'Dad!'

Still no answer.

No matter how much I shouted.

Pulling the neck of my hoody over my mouth and nose, I pushed the door back and cautiously made my way into the kitchen. *Phew!* Despite the smoke, there was no sign of an actual fire. I turned off the oven and, skirting the old tin bathtub piled high with LARP weapons, flung open the back door. Grabbing Dad's *Stranger Things* T-shirt from the pile of washing next to the machine, I wafted at the smoke alarm until it finally stopped. What was Dad playing at? He was always getting distracted, but this was something else. He could have burnt the house down.

Bracing myself, I opened the oven. Pizza

massacre or what. It was like something out of a horror movie. The dough balls had turned to charcoal, and the pizza had sagged and fallen through the rack, transforming into a low-lurking tar monster. I was never going to be able to clean that off the bottom of the oven. Anyway, Dad could do it. Where was he? Disappearing with food left in the oven was bad even by his standards!

Batting away wisps of smoke, I trotted over to the ancient writing bureau in the living room and pressed the speed dial on the landline. The *Lord of the Rings* theme tune drifted from the porch, where Dad's phone vibrated on the windowsill next to his keys. So much for that idea. Maybe he was in the shed or something? He often disappeared into a time warp when he was making LARP props.

But Dad wasn't in the shed.

Or the back garden.

Gravel poking through my chipmunk slippers, I wandered back round to the front of the house, pausing to look at the wispy mist tickling the top of the hills. Wherever Dad had gone, let's hope he was back soon, because the fog closed in quickly around here.

'What you up to, hanging around by the road?'

Mrs Burden. She was standing by the bubbling spring at the bottom of her garden. How did she do that? It was like she just appeared out of thin air sometimes.

'Well?' She crossed her arms over her flowery quilted housecoat.

'I'm not up to anything, Mrs Burden, honest.'

'How come the chickens are so upset then?'

'Pardon?'

'The chickens. Couldn't hear me programmes for all their fussing.'

I glanced over at the chicken coop. They were a bit noisier than usual I suppose. But nowhere near as noisy as Mrs Burden's giant telly. With her front door wide open, you could probably hear it in Hexham.

'Maybe there's a fox or something,' I said.

'Mmm, well that would be convenient, wouldn't it?'

Not for the chickens. Not for anyone, in fact, but Mrs Burden never let the truth get in the way of a good telling-off.

'Go on, then,' she said. 'Hurry up back inside. There's rain on the way.'

'I don't think so—'

A fat raindrop, the size of a fifty-pence piece, landed on my T-shirt. It was followed by another. And another.

Mrs Burden tightened the chiffon headscarf she wore over her rollers and tapped her nose. 'See,' she said. 'Felt it in my waterworks.'

Back inside the cottage, the TV blurred, grainy images of Roman legionaries flickering in and out of focus. Dad must have been watching one of his old movies again. Some of the soldiers appeared to be made of lava. They stood firm, shields raised, as a cavalry unit led by a bare-chested centaur wearing surfer beads charged towards them. What a load of rubbish!

I pressed the stop button on the remote, but

nothing happened. The TV refused to turn off too – no matter how many times I tried. Maybe the DVD player had overridden it or something? Dad had recently bought it second-hand from Mrs Burden, and it had been playing up since day one. I knelt down on the rug, pressing each of the buttons in turn.

Nothing.

Except for the volume increasing. Like, really!

Reaching behind the pine cabinet, I flicked the switch off at the plug. At last, the TV screen turned black.

But then it flashed back into life again. The weird lava army had been replaced by a close-up of a little boy wearing a pristine white toga. He held his hand out towards me as though inviting me to join him in the deserted Roman forum where he was loitering behind a marble column. I pulled the plug out of the wall and the image froze, the creepy boy staring out at me like something from your worst nightmare. Still, I had at least managed to kill the sound. Which would have to do for now.

My stomach was growling like my French teacher when someone forgets their homework. I never did my best thinking on an empty stomach. And my stomach was majorly empty.

Mouth watering at the thought of the fish and chips and giant ice cream sundaes the twins had no doubt demolished by now, I made my way into the kitchen. Dad better have a good explanation for all of this – especially given the lack of food in the cupboards. There had to be something that didn't need to go in the minging oven.

In the end, I settled on beans on toast with a fried apple garnish. Not my brightest idea – it would seem there's a reason why people don't serve singed fruit with their beans – but I fancied something exotic. Shovelling the last of the toast into my mouth, I scraped what was left of the apple into the bin and stacked the plate next to the sink with the breakfast and lunch dishes.

Eww. I grimaced as my hand brushed against a meaty bluebottle that was doing an Oscar-winning performance of the dying fly. Poor thing. I had to put it out of its misery. The rolled-up copy of *Tabletop Gaming* weighed heavy in my hand. *Mmm, maybe I should give it some sugar water instead.* You know, like you do with bees. I scoured the worktops for the sugar bowl—

The teaspoon clattered to the floor as music blasted from the living room – an eerie folk song that appeared to be being sung by a cat being wrung through a mangle. The TV again! What was going on?

CHAPTER 7

MRS BURDEN'S LAMB FRIES

Fingers rammed firmly in my ears, I stared at the flickering TV screen. Looking back, maybe I should have given more thought to how it was working with no power, but I was too busy trying to work out how a cute little boy with ringlets could make such a demonic sound. That was it – I couldn't be doing with that all night. I was going to have to go and ask Mrs Burden how to switch the DVD player off before my ears turned themselves inside out.

The sun was sinking behind the hilltops as I made my way outside, the fog coming off the moors a weird shade of turquoise. It wasn't dark enough for the security light to kick in, but daylight was definitely slipping away. Brow furrowed, I glanced over in the direction of the Rome Play site. It really wasn't like Dad to leave me on my own this late.

Rubbing my goosebumped arms, I scurried across the gravel and opened the gate leading into Mrs Burden's garden. The shutters were wide open, and I could see her head poking above the surprisingly modern leather couch. Images of rolling hills flashed on her massive flat-screen TV. I just hoped she wasn't watching *Emmerdale* – she once burst my football with a carving knife because it hit her window during *Emmerdale*. I rang the doorbell and braced myself as she opened the door.

'What is it, lass?'

The Burdens' Bedlington terrier, Kevin, shot out from behind her. He jumped up at me and licked my hand, his tail wagging furiously. I love Kevin. He's the only member of the Burden family who actually seems to like me.

'Hello, there,' I said, bending down and tickling his woolly tummy. He was a funny little thing. More like a lamb that had been washed on the hot cycle with a stray black sock than a dog—

'Ahem.'

I stood up, trying not to stare at Mrs Burden's nightie, which was sticking out from under her housecoat. Pleated with a gold trim, it was proper fancy.

'Well?' she said.

'I'm sorry to bother you, but—'

'Spit it out, will yer? Bert's plating up me **lamb fries**.'

Kevin looked up at me encouragingly, his floppy ear cocked.

'It's the DVD player,' I said.

'What of it?'

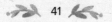

'It won't turn off.'

Mrs Burden folded her arms, lips pinched. 'Broke it already? Have you people got no respect for anything?'

I braced myself. Mrs Burden's 'respect' lectures were known to go on for a while, but instead of the usual verbal onslaught she simply tutted. Maybe she was ill or something?

'I think I must be doing something wrong,' I continued.

'Probably. You've never struck me as the brightest. Yer father neither. Where is he, anyway, sending a scrawny little bairn round to do his dirty work for him?'

'He had to go out.'

'Had to go out, yer say? Now where would he be going on a night like this?' Mrs Burden glanced over towards the moors and the shimmering turquoise fog. She put her hand to her mouth and took a step backwards.

'It's probably something to do with the Harry Styles concert,' I said. 'They'll be practising for the big show.'

Mrs Burden looked at me like I'd just done a wee on her foot. Kevin seemed a bit weirded out by the light too. He gave an angry growl, staring intensely at Mrs Burden.

'Don't blame me, lad,' she said. 'This is not of my making.'

'What's not of your making?'

'That's not for me to say. You go back inside now before you upset Kevin any further.'

Kevin did seem pretty agitated. But how was that my fault?

'So, the DVD player . . . ?' I said.

'Leave it, dog,' Mrs Burden said, ignoring me and wagging her finger at Kevin. 'She'll be reet. **The Fates** are on her side.'

Erg, OK. Maybe she was ill. She was acting odd even by her standards. She sighed and reached for the door handle.

'Now, if you don't mind, me lamb fries are going cold. Come on, Kev, nowt worse than cold lamb fries.'

Kevin replied with a short, sharp yap.

'Inside, Kevin. Now!'

'But the DVD player,' I said. 'I don't suppose you have a manual?'

Mrs Burden shook her head, her face solemn as she reached for Kevin's collar. 'A manual won't help you now. You just have to let it play out. You'll know by the morning what the score is.'

CHAPTER 8

WORRY WORMS

'Dad? Dad is that you?' Sitting up on the sofa, I rubbed my eyes. The glare from the TV was ridiculously bright. The DVD had eventually stopped playing after I'd whacked it with my slipper, but the boy's face remained fixed on the screen. And yes, I know, the slipper-whacking thing was probably a bit extreme, but if you'd had to listen to that singing you'd do anything to make it stop too.

'Dad?'

Nothing. I was sure I'd heard the door. Stretching out my shoulders, I glanced at the brass pendulum clock over the fireplace. Three a.m. Worry worms wriggled in my tummy. Something bad must have happened – Dad would never leave me on my own overnight. I threw back the patchwork blanket—

There was a whirring sound and the television flashed. *No way!* The DVD had started to play again. Please no, I couldn't take any more of the boy's singing! Thankfully, he was too busy trying to calm a rather agitated-looking dog . . .

A small curly-haired dog . . .

. . . that looked . . .

. . . just like Kevin.

Gravel scrunched underfoot.

And the security light burst into life.

'Get 'ere, dog,' yelled Mrs Burden.

Knock.

Knock.

Knock.

No way.

This could not be happening.

Knock.

Knock.

Knock.

But somehow it was.

Heart pounding, I pulled back the curtain. And there he was. The boy from the video.

'Well, open the door,' he said, his chin-length hair falling in perfect strawberry blonde ringlets around his face. He must have been strong, because the replica Roman torch he was carrying was almost as big as him.

I shuffled behind the curtain. Sure, he was like Year 1 max and looked like a cherub, but a minute ago he was on my telly. There was something majorly weird going on.

'Come, Silvia.' The boy turned on his heel. 'Romana needs you.'

Romana? Hold on a minute – a boy in a tunic

and a strange Roman-sounding name? This had to be something to do with Rome Play.

'Wait!' I called, grappling with the door keys. 'Wait!'

I flung the door open.

The boy was gone.

Shivering, I scanned the driveway. The thick fog had lifted, leaving behind a wispy ground mist. It whirled and swirled around the garden.

'Hello?'

Clouds raced across the glimmering moon. At the bottom of the drive, I saw a ghostly figure carrying a dimly lit torch. 'Hurry, Silvia. It is time.'

I curled my hands into tight fists. What was Dad playing at? Was he really expecting me to go traipsing around after some little kid in the middle of the night? I know he'd said he had some big surprises planned, but this was taking things too far!

'Wait! Where's my dad?'

But the boy was already crossing the road.

'Come back,' I called, legging it after him.

Laughter drifted towards me – a mischievous giggle that seemed to be mocking me. Dad was so in for it when I found him.

'Stop! Wait for me!' I followed the floating light of the boy's torch. 'Please wait!'

But the boy continued heading into the darkness, his torch flickering in and out of view as he made his way up the hill towards Hadrian's Wall and the distant turquoise glow.

CHAPTER 9

STOP PLAY!

Staring into the darkness ten minutes later, panic rose in my chest. There was no sign of the boy. Or anyone else. What was going on?

My trainers soaking from the damp grass, I continued in the direction of Housesteads Fort. Dad had to be around here somewhere. Surely even he wouldn't be daft enough to have me wandering through the valley on my own in the dark?

The torchlight again.

'Stop play!' I called.

The moon broke through the cloud, casting strange shadows on the hillside. The boy's toga shimmered.

'Stop the game right now!'

I picked up pace, but the boy seemed to take this as an invitation to go faster, the gap between us getting wider and wider. Seriously, he was superfast. And I mean, like, Ferrari fast. Whereas I was more Vauxhall Corsa. Stumbling on the uneven surface, I raced on, the sinking feeling in my stomach growing stronger with every step.

'This is so not funny, Dad!'

And like things weren't bad enough, I could hear cows. Never trust a cow. They may look cute but believe me, they're evil. You can tell by their eyes. They're all the same colour – BROWN. Never blue. Never green. Never grey. Just

BROWN. Think about it . . . ! But don't think about it for too long because there's a lot going on right now and you don't want to lose track of things.

A sudden wind whipped at my hair. In the distance I heard voices. Grown-up voices.

'Dad!' I yelled. 'Is that you?'

No response. Except for the cows, who mooed louder, as though to tell me to be quiet. Which was fair enough, I suppose. It was late and they did have calves.

Yikes, they have calves!

Everyone knows that's when they're at their most evil. Feet squelching in the thick mud, I tried to make myself as small as possible, and continued forward.

Voices again.

And another shadowy glimpse of the boy as he disappeared over the brow of the hill.

'Hello?'

Thunder roared in the distance and the turquoise glow flashed brighter, making the darkness that followed all the more terrifying.

'Hello, is there anybody there?'

Another clap of thunder.

Turquoise lightning split the sky.

Like, what the gladiator sandals! The imposing triumphal arch seemed to have appeared from nowhere. Kenzo was not wrong when he said his creation was going to take things to a whole new level! But how could I not have noticed it, especially as it was lit by what had to be the biggest fire cauldron in the world?

Raised high above the ground on a bronze pedestal, the cauldron flickered white, turquoise and purple. Around the base of the pedestal, about shoulder-high, there was a ring of flaming torches.

Lightning flashed again, turning the clouds an electric blue.

Above the roar of the cauldron, I heard laughter.

There was shouting too and a low rumble, which sounded like a horse and cart travelling over cobbles.

Yet all I could see through the archway was darkness.

A darkness that swallowed me as I stepped over the threshold.

CHAPTER 10

THE HORSEMAN

ike, what? How was this even possible? In the space of just a few hours, the forlorn wooden buildings I'd seen earlier had been transformed into a full-on reconstruction of a Roman town. The crew must have been on turbocharge or something! If this was basic, I'd love to see what Kenzo did on a big budget, because this set made

Disneyland look like it had been built by our school drama group. No wonder it had brought in the crowds.

Where had they all come from? We hadn't even opened yet and dudes in tunics and capes were literally spilling out of the tavern up ahead. Dad was not lying when he said the pre-party was going to create a huge buzz! But wasn't it supposed to be tomorrow?

Picking my jaw back up off the ground, I continued along the paved street towards the tavern. *Yes, paved. The street was paved?* And that wasn't the only odd thing – the whole set-up seemed different. It was hard to see in the dim light, but everything felt bigger . . . a LOT bigger . . .

Wishing I had a torch, I zigzagged my way around the rowdy men in tunics. Like, what was with all the funny looks? Sure, I got it. It was a bit of a no-no to wear normal clothes at a LARP, but the dude in the dangerously short tunic was staring at me like I'd just stolen his last chip. You'd think he'd never seen a pair of trackie bottoms before.

And why was it suddenly so hot? The place stank too: rotten veg and portaloos with a hint of something else I couldn't quite make out—

'Out of my way, vagabond!'

Slipping on a random chicken carcass, I darted out of the path of a purple-caped soldier on a horse. 'Well excuse you!' The numpty had almost run me over.

The soldier turned his horse, circling me like a buzzard sussing out its prey. His intricately carved helmet glimmering in the moonlight, he spat on the ground near my feet.

Like, no need! I hope one of the **gamemasters** saw it! He'd be out of the game.

'You,' he bawled. 'You dare hold my eye?'

And the sooner he was out, the better. He was taking himself far too seriously. With the dark shadows of the street and the gleaming dagger on his hip, it was all starting to feel a bit too real. Well, except for his luminous teeth – no way were those bad boys natural.

'Kneel! Now!'

I don't think so. The stone paving was filthy. I held my hand above my head to signal I was out of game and edged backwards.

'Insolent **plebeian**. It is not wise to provoke me!'

Really? Was he still going on? Maybe Dad had decided on a different signal? Still, the trackie bottoms made it kind of obvious I wasn't in character.

Thankfully he was distracted by another soldier. This dude had no respect for health and safety either, as he charged towards us on a foaming chestnut horse. No wonder horses aren't normally allowed at LARP events. I'd never been so scared for my toes in my life.

'Hail!' he shouted, slowing his horse. 'Bellona has spoken. It is time.'

It is time? That's what the boy had said too. Well, it was definitely about time Dad put in an appearance! I'd had enough. I was hot, thirsty and tired and this just wasn't funny any more. Not that it ever really was. How could Dad think this was OK? He was so in for it when I found him.

The soldiers deep in whispered conversation – something about spies and mavericks from what I could work out – I darted behind a passing cart and legged it down the street, the road opening up on to a shadowy piazza. Wow! It was epic! I mean, I'm talking full-on Roman forum here, guys. **Basilica**. Temple. **Senate House**. The lot! In fact, it was all a little too epic . . .

I'd been too busy worrying about the horseman to take it all in before, but the more I studied my surroundings, the more real they seemed. Kenzo was good, the best special effects person around, but he wasn't a miracle worker. There was no way he could have transformed those sad-looking plywood buildings I'd seen earlier into this.

Sticking to the shadows, I edged my way along a rust-coloured tenement. Columned buildings as tall as Newcastle Library loomed over me—

Whoa, what was that? It sounded like a baby crying.

Neck hairs rising, I looked up at the tenement, locking eyes with a shadowy figure in one of the windows. No way, there were people living in there!

Worry worms doing a breakdance, I ran my fingers over the building facade.

Brick – actual brick?

Not plywood or polystyrene like you'd expect.

Brick!

What was going on?

CHAPTER 11

MORE SURPRISES

Hugging my arms tight across my chest, I leant back against the wall, trying to make sense of my surroundings. So, if this wasn't the Rome Play site – which it couldn't possibly be – where was I—

'Vagabond!'

Uh-oh! The angry dude on the horse again!

That was all I needed.

Hooves pounding, he cantered towards me, one hand on the reins, the other reaching for his leather whip. 'Come here, plebeian,' he called. 'I will not ask twice.'

Like that was going to happen! I had no idea what was happening here, but I did know I was going nowhere near that Caligula wannabe. Heart pounding, I looked around for somewhere to hide as the horseman's whip sent a waft of air towards my ankles.

'**Asine nebulo!**' he cried.

Donkey trash? What a charmer.

'Here. Now! I am not done with you yet.'

Well, I was most definitely done with him. Breathing in short, sharp rasps, I ran into the dark shadows of the forum. With the temple looming at the far end of the market square, and the imposing basilica to my left, it was just like being inside one of my Roman history books. Which would have been kind of cool, except for the obvious.

'You think you can outwit me? I am Cornelius

Lucius Sulla, Head of the **Praetorian Guard**, and I will not be outdone by a plebeian in demonic costume.'

Wow, he really was a diva. And, unfortunately, a persistent one.

Gagging at the stench of rotten fish and vegetables, I darted behind the food carts, edging backwards into the shadows of the basilica where I crouched down behind one of the thick marble columns. I was far too close to the rubbish heap for my liking, but with the horseman now cantering back and forth alongside the colonnade it seemed safer to stay put. Hopefully, he'd get bored and go away.

Though it didn't look like that was happening any time soon. If anything, with the rhythmic thud of hooves echoing off the walls, it sounded like he was closing in on me.

'My patience is waning, child. Do not make me hunt you down like the street rat that you are.'

Holding my breath, I poked my head out to take another look. He was so close I could smell the earthy scent of the horse. I counted to ten to calm my breathing and focused on keeping still.

'So be it.' The horseman climbed down from the saddle. He paused and sniffed the air. He'd noticed it too. The earthy scent had grown stronger – my nostrils filled with the scent of damp moors and heather.

Cape swirling, the horseman put his hand to his sword. 'Halt! Who goes there?'

Something moved in the shadows.

Something fuzzy.

Woolly even?

It charged at the horseman, yapping and yipping.

No way! Kevin!

And like that wasn't weird enough, there was Mrs Burden too. She'd lost the housecoat and was wearing a long pleated dress with a gold trim around the hem. Was that her nightie? She still had her headscarf on, though, and her rollers in – which is the only way I could tell it was her. There were none of the usual sharp edges and frown lines and she was glowing like an angel. A supercharged angel who smelt of fresh air and early spring mornings on the moors.

'What yer staring at?!' she spat at the wide-mouthed horseman. 'Never seen a goddess before?'

Goddess!!!

Mrs Burden!

Like, what?

The horseman bowed his head and knelt down on one knee, like a shepherd who'd just seen the Angel Gabriel.

'On yer feet, you pumpkin!' Mrs Burden crossed her arms. 'Picking on little kids! Back to base like yer were told!'

'Of course, oh divine one.'

Divine one? Really?

The soldier wiped a fish head off his knee. 'And as soon as permitted, I shall return and sacrifice a chicken in your honour, mighty **Coventina**.'

Coventina? The goddess of wells and springs. Well, it explained the spring in her garden, I suppose.

'A chicken?' spat Mrs Burden.

Kevin growled.

'A small goat, then. Perhaps that's more to your liking?'

'Stick yer chicken and yer goat.' Mrs Burden crossed her arms, a cloud of steam rising from her ears. And I'm not using a metaphor here like teachers make you do in creative writing lessons. This was real-life actual steam like what comes out of the kettle. Only it smelt nice. Proper nice, like those fancy scented reeds they have in the toilets at posh cafes.

'Times are hard, oh divine one,' continued the horseman. 'I fear I have angered **Fortuna**. You couldn't have a word, could you?'

'Have a word? *Have a word?*'

Kevin lay down and covered his eyes with his paws.

'Get out of here before you feel the wrath of Coventina too! You have no idea what yer meddling with!'

Brow furrowed, the guard bowed his head and backed towards his horse. Climbing into the saddle, he nodded in my direction. 'Is that her?' he asked. 'The one the prophecy speaks of? I meant no offence—'

'No offence!' Mrs Burden said, spitting a powerful jet of water that made the horse caterpillar like a breakdancer. 'Begone, before I make my own sacrifice.'

Mrs Burden watched the horseman set off across the square. 'A chicken,' she scoffed, shaking her head. 'A measley chicken! This is what happens when you're sent to the sticks.'

'The sticks?' Cautiously, I edged closer towards her. She was scary at the best of times, but this had just taken things to a whole new level.

'Outposts, *she* calls them.' Mrs Burden looked over at the temple and frowned. 'She keeps us there, just in case.'

'Just in case what?'

'Someone gets through the gateway, of course. The realms aren't supposed to mix.'

The realms? Honestly, my head was about to explode.

'She won't be happy about this, you know. You roaming around Romana City, drawing attention to yourself. Still, it's her own fault, trusting Felix to carry the torch and bring you in.'

'Who won't be happy? Mrs Burden, what is going on? Am I dreaming?' I had to be, right?

'Dreaming? You wish!' Mrs Burden looked over to the temple at the far end of the forum. 'Right, come on, Kevin. Bert will be doing his nut wondering where we are.'

Kevin's short, sharp yaps echoed around us.

'Stop it, dog! I told you, this is none of our business.'

Kevin clearly thought otherwise. He trotted towards me defiantly. I reached down to stroke him, almost jumping out of my skin as Mrs Burden fired a jet of cold water from her hand, soaking my T-shirt.

'Don't you be encouraging him. He's disobedient enough.' She clicked her fingers. 'Now move it, Kevin. Do as yer told or you'll never see another plate of lamb fries and gravy again.'

Kevin sighed and shook the water out of his woolly coat. He stared up at Mrs Burden.

'Don't be guilting me now, dog. It's the only way if she wants to find her father.'

'Dad – do you know where he is? Mrs Burden, please? Tell me what this is all about. Where am I?'

'Kevin! Now!' Mrs Burden undid her gold necklace and hooked it on to Kevin's collar. When he refused to budge, she bent down and whispered in his ear. He looked at me, tail drooped, whimpering one last time before allowing Mrs Burden to lead him away.

'But you can't just leave me here. You have to help me find Dad. What if that Cornelius fella comes back? How will you live with yourself if he murders me in cold blood?'

'Oh, give over, lass.' But Mrs Burden looked more sad than angry. 'Like it or not, my path takes me home. You'll be reet. Trust your gut, the Fates will look after the rest—'

'Coventina!' Creepy torch boy again! His torch cast long eerie shadows around us. 'What are you doing here? Does Mamma know you're in Romana?'

'No, lad, and probably best she doesn't. Still, I won't tell her you left the gateway to Britannia open if you don't.'

The boy's skin glowed yellow in the lantern light. 'But I shut it, I'm sure I did.'

'Well, how come Kevin got through, then? Thought I'd lost him, I did. Had to come in after him.'

The boy scratched his head like he was thinking really hard. 'But I'm certain . . . naughty Coventina, are you trying to trick me?'

'Tricks? Do you think I've got time for tricks while me hot milk's going cold back home? Now off you go. And remember, not a word of this to anyone . . . not unless you want your mother to send you back to the naughty cloud.' Mrs Burden crossed her arms. 'Not that you didn't deserve it last time. Poor Bert nearly lost an eye helping me to track that cyclops you let through.'

The boy scowled and held his hand out towards

me. 'Come on, then,' he said. 'Before we both get in trouble.'

'Erg, I don't think so.'

'Go with Felix, Silvia,' said Mrs Burden, shaking her head. 'There's no stopping this now.'

CHAPTER 12

ALONE

And that was that! Mrs Burden had gone. Vanished in a cloud of fragrant steam and taken Kevin with her. Brilliant! Not! What was I going to do now?

'Don't be sad,' said the boy – Felix. 'Come on, let's go and get some honey cake.'

'Honey cake? My dad is missing. I have no idea

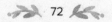

where I am or why I'm here. And you want to go for cake?'

'It's really nice. Mamma had it made specially for your arrival.' He took my hand. 'And you're in Romana, of course. Come on – we need to get back before Mamma does. She's already in a nark. It's because of Vulcan—'

I shook my hand free. 'Sorry, but I need to go and find my dad.'

'Yes,' said the boy. 'Mamma is going to help you.'

I looked over to the tavern, where a brawl had broken out. Unfamiliar buildings loomed above and the darkness seemed to wrap itself around me. Suddenly I felt very alone.

Tired.

Hungry.

Confused.

And alone.

Maybe taking time out to have a piece of honey cake with a superstrong boy who knew this Romana place wasn't such a bad idea?

'Can your mum really help me find my dad?'

73

'Yes,' said the boy. 'If anyone can, Mamma can. Come on, Silvia. Race you to the temple!'

He sprinted across the forum and up the temple steps, the giant cauldrons either side of the panelled wooden doors bursting into life.

'I thought we were going to your house?' I said, catching him up.

'We are.' He banged on the temple door and tutted. 'Looks like we'll have to use the side entrance. The **Bellonari** must be skiving again. They're supposed to look after me when Mamma's not here, but they usually just sit in the **piscina** gossiping and feasting.'

'You live in the temple?'

'Of course, where else would we live? Come on.'

Trainers squeaking on the marble floor, I followed Felix across the **portico** to the side of the temple, the colonnade giving way to the smooth walls of the **domus**. He stopped and put his lantern down outside a purple wooden door, sandwiched between two shuttered **tabernae**.

'They're probably using the key boy for target

practice again,' he frowned, banging his fist against the door. 'Open up, you lot, or I'll tell Mamma you locked me out!'

Metal scraped against wood and the door creaked open to reveal a squat man with a bald head. Water dripped from his white toga, forming a puddle on the mosaic floor. 'And I'll tell her you lost the Undecided.'

'Did not.' Felix nodded his head in my direction. 'And anyway, we're not supposed to mention any of that stuff.'

'Oops.' The priest gave me a mischievous wink. 'Are you coming in or what? No doubt our important guest is hungry.'

CHAPTER 13

THE DOMUS

The corridor led into a lofty atrium. Moonlight shone through the opening in the roof, lighting up the water feature in the centre of the room. The walls were covered in marble work and **frescoes**, and the panelled ceiling was loaded with intricate mouldings of the gods. It was all a bit OTT if you asked me – even by Roman standards.

As for the giant statues, like, no need. Especially the one of the fierce-looking war goddess Bellona. A marble chariot in your living room. What was that all about?

Not that I had time to take it all in properly. Not with Felix walking so fast. I followed him further into the house, catching glimpses of the curtained bedchambers and living spaces. It was well posh. Felix's mum must be mega important living in a gaff like this. Maybe she really could help me find Dad?

She also had a serious obsession with Bellona. Admiring the life-sized fresco of the auburn-haired goddess nursing a baby centaur, I breathed in the sweet incense and made my way outside into the **peristyle** garden. May as well have some of that honey cake while I waited for her. I was starving, and my tongue was so dry you could have used it to sole a gladiator sandal.

'Want to get in the piscina?' Felix said.

Erg, no thank you. Sure, the shallow pool in the centre of the courtyard looked inviting, but there were three very nosy priests sitting in it.

'Is that her, then?' said the oldest priest. Like the others, he wore a gold laurel wreath above his ears. 'Bit scrawny.'

'Don't be so judgemental, Linus,' said the priest who'd opened the door. 'And anyway, we'll soon feed her up.' He held out the platter of sweetmeats he was balancing on his belly. 'Want one of these, **pupa**? I'm Cassius and these are my esteemed colleagues, Linus and Juba.'

'You shouldn't call her doll,' said the third priest. 'It's patronizing.'

'Oh, get over yourself. She doesn't mind, do you, pupa? Gallio, pour her some wine! Does nobody in this place understand the divine duty of **hospitium**?'

'Wine? I'm twelve.'

The older priest adjusted his laurel wreath. 'And your point is?'

'Leave it, Linus!' said Cassius. 'Remember, while we have long anticipated her arrival, the Undecided is unaccustomed to our ways.'

The Undecided thing again? Why did he keep calling me that? I guess I was a bit indecisive. Especially when it came to pizza toppings. But how would he know?

'So, Silvia,' continued Cassius, 'about that wine. Perhaps you would like Gallio to add a little extra water?'

'Erg, actually, could I just have the water please? And it's Livi. Nobody calls me Silvia.'

'OK, Silvia. But I really wouldn't recommend the water without some form of tonic. I caught Linus weeing in the **impluvium** earlier—'

'Slander!' The older priest waved his arm in the air in protest.

Cassius shrugged apologetically and climbed out of the piscina. 'Come, Silvia. We have sacrificed a bull in anticipation of your arrival. Can't beat a bit of bull meat and cheese.'

I stared at the banqueting table under the red-tiled peristyle. A giant bull's head stared back, the stench of chargrilled flesh and unfamiliar herbs turning my stomach.

'Thanks,' I said. 'But I've already eaten. When will your mum be back, Felix?'

'Soon. She should have been here by now.'

'I wouldn't count on it,' said Cassius, piling his bronze platter high with bull meat and shellfish. 'She's gathering reinforcements. Word is the fire god is ready to strike.' He hid his mouth with his hand. 'Glad I'm not the one who has to stop this.'

Seriously, what was with the hand over mouth thing? Did he think I was completely clueless!

'I can hear you, you know. What are you going on about?'

Cassius looked at Felix, who was chewing his thumb.

'Mamma will explain everything,' he said, his face pale in the lamplight. 'She will help you end this.'

I shook my head. Fire gods? Prophecies? And weeing in the water supply? Could this lot be any more ridiculous? And I doubted Felix's mum would be any better. What was I going to do . . . ?

Trust your gut, that's what Mrs Burden had said.

Use your intuition. Well, my intuition was telling me to get out of there. At least I think it was my intuition – it could have been the burnt apple garnish from earlier. Either way I had an uneasy feeling in my stomach and wanted out.

'Erg, OK,' I said. 'Good luck with it all. I'm going to find my dad.'

'Please, Silvia. Mamma says Vulcan is expecting you to go to him.'

I stood up, but Felix grabbed my hand. 'You can't leave. You are in great danger.'

Maybe, but if the alternative was staying here with this lot, I was prepared to take my chances.

CHAPTER 14

ROME, BUT NOT AS WE KNOW IT!

The sun was just beginning to rise as I hurried out of the temple and back to the forum. I gave myself a moment to take it all in: the senate house with its whirring weathervane and sundial clock, the four-storey basilica where yawning shop-keepers creaked open intricately carved bronze shutters, and in the distance, [illegible] the oval amphithcatre with its [illegible] arches and billboards. It was Ancie[illegible] not how we know it.

It was the little things, mainly, tha[illegible] it different to the computer-generated reconstructions I'd seen online – things like the freestanding carved-bronze noticeboards loaded with tatty flyers, and the metal water sculpture with its whirling cogs and gladiators. Things I hadn't noticed in the dark. Gulls screeched above and the smell of baking bread fought to defeat the stench of the open drains—

'Silvia,' called Felix behind me. 'Come back.'

I continued past the drinking fountain, where a pint-sized girl collected water from a serpent's mouth.

'Please, Silvia! You're going to get me in trouble.' Felix was right beside me now, pleading at me with his big brown eyes. 'Mamma will lose it if you're not there when she gets home.'

I felt bad for him. I honestly did – trapped there

...se joker priests at the temple, but right now ...had to focus on finding Dad. Maybe afterwards I could come back and help him in some way.

I paused as a bunch of guards in white tunics marched purposefully across the forum, the plumes on their fancy-pants helmets swaying in the breeze. At the front of the senate house, they split into pairs and began to bang papyrus posters into anything that would take a nail.

'Oh dear,' said Felix. 'What now?'

'Only one way to find out!' I waited for the guards to move on and trotted over to the nearest board.

Curfew! said the newly posted papyrus. But it wasn't the news of the evening lockdown that bothered me. It was the hand-drawn mugshots plastered all over the board under the headline – *The stolen!* Honestly, there were loads of them. And slap bang in the middle of the mosaic of startled faces was a picture of Dad!

Yes, Dad. My dad!

'Are you all right, Silvia?'

All-write. I was so far from all-write I couldn't even spell it.

'Sorry,' Felix said. 'He's a lava soldier. They all are.'

'What?'

'Vulcan. He's been stealing people for his lava army. He's assembling his forces in the north of Romana, just like the prophecy foretold.'

'How do I get to the north?'

'It's too dangerous, Silvia.'

Perhaps, but I had to try!

'We have to wait for Mamma.'

In the far corner of the forum, I noticed a metal shelter with a slogan painted on the back:

Mercury Cart
The easiest way to travel!

'That'll do nicely.'

'What are you doing?' Felix grabbed my T-shirt. 'You can't take the Mercury Cart. It's for plebeians.'

I shook myself free. What a snob! I know he's only little, but still. 'In case you haven't noticed, I'm a plebeian too. We can't all live in fancy houses with statues and swimming pools in the garden.'

Felix began to giggle. He ran along beside me. 'You're so funny, Silvia. Of course you're not a plebeian, you're—' Stopping mid-sentence, he glanced over my shoulder, his brow furrowing. 'Uh-oh! We're in for it now.'

Whoa, what was that! The turquoise blur was plummeting towards us like a missile. A super-charged missile on a supercharged missile mega mission. I backed away, searching for the safest place to shelter, but then stopped. The missile was slowing. The blur not quite so blurry.

I rubbed my eyes. *You've got to be kidding me!*

Horses!

Flying horses!

Four of them, pulling an intricately carved racing chariot, which landed with a thud that made my teeth chatter. Market traders and early-morning shoppers fell to their knees, bodies lowered to the floor in the direction of the ruby-embossed golden chariot.

'**Salve!**' said the blur.

There was a popping noise and a fizz and the turquoise haze turned to a wispy iridescent mist that drifted across the forum. No way! The chariot was being driven by a woman. A strong athletic woman with flaming auburn hair and a turquoise-plumed helmet just like in the frescoes in the temple. Bellona!

Head bowed, Felix hurried towards her. 'I'm sorry, Mamma—'

Mamma . . . ?

Bellona took off her helmet, her auburn hair glistening in the early-morning sun. She saluted Felix. 'At ease, soldier. You did not lose sight of the target. A successful mission, I'd say.'

In the space of a few milliseconds, Felix went from worry to surprise to looking like he'd just won a lifetime supply of honey cake. He threw his arms around Bellona, but she pushed him away.

'Stand down, General! What have I told you? Cuddling is for the weak.' She smiled at me and shrugged. 'Can't stand all that soppy stuff. How about you, Silvia? Ben was a bit of a sop, as I remember.'

Oh my gods. Oh my gods. Oh my gods. Dad was the biggest sop ever.

'In you get now, both of you.'

Oh my gods. Oh my gods. Oh my gods. This couldn't be happening!

Bellona huffed impatiently. 'Forward march, now, Silvia. I have news about your father.'

'You do? The poster says he's a lava soldier!' I stepped closer to the chariot but then paused. My intuition was going to my stomach again.

Bellona cracked her knuckles. 'Honestly, Silvia, you do not have to be undecided about everything!'

Felix giggled. He threw his arms around Bellona again. 'Funny Mamma! Can we go and have some honey cake now?'

'Of course,' said Bellona, peeling his arms from around her waist. 'Just as soon as your sister realizes who's in command and marches on into the chariot. Fall in, now, Silvia. Do as Mamma tells you.'

CHAPTER 15

MAMMA'S GIRL

Erg, hello? Did I hear that right?

Bellona.

Goddess of War.

Claiming to be my mum?

What a load of rubbish! If I was a demigod, I think I'd have realized it by now. I wouldn't come last every time we did cross-country, for a start.

What to do?

What to do?

Maybe if I closed my eyes and ignored her this would all go away.

'Silvia, in the chariot, now!'

So much for that idea.

'Honestly, why do you have to turn everything into a battle?'

Bit rich coming from the Goddess of War. Seriously, this couldn't be happening.

'Come, on the double! I know this is uncharted territory, but I'll explain everything over a glorious slice of honey cake.'

'Honey cake!' Felix thumped the air. 'Come on, sis!'

'Don't call me that!'

Brain whirling, I backed away, tripping over a man in a rough woollen tunic who'd fallen on to his knees in worship behind me. The shopkeepers in the basilica were now kneeling for Bellona too. And a small child with a donkey who'd appeared from nowhere.

Bellona sighed. 'Oh, Silvia, I know this is a lot to take in, but you have to trust me.'

No chance! Even if she was my mum – which she absolutely wasn't. I turned towards the metal shelter where the Mercury Cart was approaching.

'Look, Silvia, I recognize we have a few issues to resolve, but the family is a battalion. Together we will retrieve your father and free Romana from Vulcan's tyranny.'

'All hail Bellona!' exclaimed the genuflecting man in front of me. 'The saviour of Romana!'

Bellona waved her spear. 'The longer Ben is in Vulcan's clutches, the less likely it is we can save him. We must strike now or face certain doom!'

Erg, OK. Someone's been having drama lessons. I turned around and surveyed the square. It was so quiet you could hear a pin drop.

I bit my lip.

What if this was real?

I suppose it wouldn't hurt to have a war goddess on my side. The locals certainly seemed to rate her. It was like the whole world had stopped for Bellona.

'I am not the enemy here.' Bellona tapped the side of her chariot with her spear. 'Now, in you get.' She sighed, her aura shimmering. 'How is Ben, by the way? I mean apart from the obvious. Does he ever talk about me?'

My disbelief turned to anger. How dare she pretend to care about Dad. 'You abandoned us. We talk about how you abandoned us—'

Bellona laced her fingers together. She stretched out her shoulders like she was warming up for a fight. 'Oh really, Silvia, now is not the time nor place. In you come before you embarrass yourself any further. Airing the family's dirty laundry in public!'

I stared her down, trying to control the tremor in my knees. There was no denying it. Her eyes were the same steel grey as mine. I could see myself reflected in them.

'Time is running out, Silvia.'

Swallowing down my apprehension, I climbed

into the chariot. Like it or not, I needed Bellona's help. Plus, I really did fancy a piece of that honey cake – nobody does their best rescuing on an empty stomach.

CHAPTER 16

CAMP BELLONA

The chariot ride was smoother than I expected. A tad windy, admittedly, and I could have done without Bellona's billowing cape smacking me in the face every two seconds but smooth all the same. Which was a good job, given we were flying at a thousand-billion kilometres per hour, hundreds of metres above the ground.

Don't be such a wuss, was all Bellona had said when I pointed out she might not win any awards for health and safety, vincit qui se vincit! *He conquers who conquers himself.*

Not that the open chariot bothered Felix. While I gripped the rail so tightly my knuckles turned white, he held his arms above his head and leant forward into the wind like a ship's figurehead.

'Look, Silvia,' he said as we left the sprawling city behind. 'Camp Bellona!'

Wow! No wonder Felix was excited – the **castra** was epic. Dominating the strip of farmland between the city and the encroaching forest, there were literally zillions of tents, pitched in perfect parallel lines around a central forum. But then I saw it. The strange orange haze beyond the forest, the distant landscape blurred by the eerie amber light.

'Vulcan's lava soldiers,' said Felix.

Like, whoa! I lurched forward as Bellona began a sudden descent towards the camp. And when I say sudden, I mean sudden. We were hurtling towards the ground like a seagull who'd just spotted a tourist with chips.

'It's all in the thighs, Silvia,' she said. 'You'll soon get the hang of it.'

Erg, OK . . . or maybe she could quit driving like we were being chased by **Mors!** Not that I said that. It's hard to say anything when your cheeks are wobbling so much they could whip cream. Talk about G-force. Or, actually, don't, because I never want to have to think about that chariot ride again.

Thankfully it was all over pretty quickly. When you're travelling at the speed of light, it doesn't take long to plummet towards near-death.

'Here we are!' Cracking her whip, Bellona pulled back on the reins, the horses slowing as suddenly as they'd accelerated. Announcing our arrival with a fierce neigh, they circled the camp and landed in the bustling **intervallum**. And when I say bustling, I mean bustling. Busy not just with soldiers but with animals too. Sheep, goats, donkeys – you name it, they were all roaming around the intervallum.

Ignoring the saluting legionaries practising their drills near the brook, Bellona steered the horses across the trampled grass towards the camp's central access road. 'So how did you enjoy your first chariot ride?' she said.

The horses settled into a steady trot and I released my grip on the rail. Wow! This place was amazing!

'Attention, soldier!' Bellona waved her hand in front of my eyes. 'Are you still with us?'

No thanks to her. Enjoy? I mean, I'd rather ride bareback on one of the cows that were milling around than endure another one of her landings. And you know how I feel about cows.

'When are we going to find Dad?'

'Just as soon as you've retrieved the arrow from the molten dragon's lair,' replied Bellona.

'Excuse me?'

'The sacred arrow forged with Jupiter's lightning bolt,' said Felix.

'Erg, OK. I'll fetch it right away then. Not.'

'The prophecy is clear, Silvia,' said Bellona. 'It is you who will decide this. Now quiet, here come your brothers.'

'My brothers?'

'Romulus! Remus!' called Felix.

I rubbed my eyes. It might have been the light, but the two figures running towards us looked . . . blue. Duck-egg blue to be precise. And their hair appeared to be dancing.

'It's not fair,' said Felix. 'Why can't I have snake hair like the twins?'

Snake hair! I have blue twin brothers with snake hair? This had to be some sort of a wind-up, right?

Bellona pulled back on the reins and the chariot jerked to a stop. 'Because you all have your own unique talents, my little general.'

'Want to know my talent, Silvia?'

'Not now, Felix,' interrupted Bellona. 'File forward. There's honey cake waiting for you in Silvia's chambers.'

'Yes!' Felix jumped down from the chariot.

'You too, Silvia. I'm sure you'll feel much better about what lies ahead once you've spent a little time with your brothers. Just remember not to look them in the eye unless they're wearing goggles. Their father was a descendent of Medusa.'

Feel better? I don't think so. Like I didn't have enough problems at school without having gorgons for brothers.

'Go on, then.' Bellona clapped her hands together. 'Chop-chop. I'll see you at sundown—'

'But we need to find Dad. You said we'd talk about it over a nice slice of honey cake.'

'Oh Silvia, stop acting so spoilt. You'll get your cake. And your dad. Meanwhile, I have a little errand to run.'

'Romulus! Remus!' Felix legged it over to the smiling twins, who looked to be about sixteen. 'Silvia's here. And she's ready to fetch the arrow and save Romana!'

'Erg, I don't think so—'

Bellona nudged me with her hip, sending me

flying out of the chariot. 'Don't make a fuss now. He's a very old dragon, probably won't even notice you're there.'

CHAPTER 17

FOOD BEFORE STRATEGY

Heat rising in my cheeks, I watched Bellona's chariot ascend. Up up up it went, racing across the mackerel sky, until it was little more than a distant smudge. Retrieve the sacred arrow from some dragon? I don't think so. There had to be another way to get Dad back.

'She does that.'

'Does what?' I turned towards the twins.

'Disappears.'

Tell me something I don't know. I smiled, trying not to stare at their wriggling snake hair. Which was impossible, so I distracted myself by looking around the camp. The soldiers seemed to be preparing for something. Legionaries queued outside the weapons store while auxiliaries, shifting supplies, kept a close eye out for stray arrows coming from the far side of the parade, where **sagittarii** fired at wooden posts.

'A little daunting, isn't it? Don't worry, you'll soon get used to it. I'm Romulus, by the way.'

'And I'm Remus.'

Talk about peas in a pod! Their thick black goggles didn't exactly help with telling them apart either. Thank goodness the polished metal breastplates they wore over their maroon tunics were different.

'Livi,' I said, trying to act like I hung out with gorgons all the time. 'Nice to meet you.'

The snakes cocked their heads, a hundred black

glassy eyes boring into me.

'Short for Silvia,' said Felix.

'Oh yes, of course,' said Romulus. 'Silvia Fortuna Juno De Luca of Once Brewed. The Undecided. Welcome, sister.'

I shook Romulus's outstretched hand. Despite being a snake-haired monster, he seemed nice, and Dad had always told me not to judge people by their appearance.

Romulus turned towards Felix, his snake hair bobbing joyfully, as he raised his arm in salute. 'Well done, brother. I knew you'd make an excellent torchbearer.'

Felix did a happy jump, proper pleased with himself.

'Just Scylla to come now,' said Remus. 'And that's all the family together.'

'What? There are more of us?' This was getting silly. Just how many brothers and sisters did I have?

'Yes,' said Remus. 'You'll meet everyone later at the celebration feast. Though I wouldn't expect much in way of conversation from Scylla.'

'She's a sea monster,' Felix giggled. 'Mum's gone to fetch her. She thought she might be a bit much for me to collect, what with her six heads and all.'

Like, could today get any weirder? Watching Remus's snake hair nod in agreement, a thought struck me. Maybe I was sick? Hallucinating like that time I had a high temperature and told Dad I'd seen a leprechaun floating past the window eating a Mr Whippy. Or maybe it was the fumes from the burnt pizza messing with my mind? One thing I did know, hallucination or not, I wasn't hanging around for no celebration dinner. How could they even talk of such a thing with everything that was going on?

'Now now, Felix.' Romulus smiled. 'I fear we are overwhelming sister. Come, Silvia, you must be in need of some refreshment after this most eventful morning.'

'Honey cake,' bellowed Felix. 'Let's go and have some honey cake!'

'Sorry, it's lovely to meet you and all that,' I said, 'but I have to go and find my dad.'

'Of course, sister.' Remus drew his sword. 'But food before strategy. Hospitium demands it.' He winked at Felix and held his sword out in front of him. 'Oppugna!' *Charge!*

'I have to go now!' I insisted.

But Remus was already halfway across the parade. Tugging Felix's tunic playfully, he legged it past him and disappeared into a large purple tent. The door flaps were pulled open, and I could see the servants inside jumping to attention, loading the low tables with platters piled high with food.

'Please, sister,' said Romulus. 'I understand you wish to find your father, but you must be patient. The Prima **Sibyl** has spoken. The only way to end this and bring peace to Romana is for you to retrieve the arrow.'

'I don't believe in prophecy.' And I definitely wasn't having it that some ancient prophetess had me down as the saviour of this Romana place. 'We decide our own future.'

That's what the motivational poster in our deputy head's office said, anyway. He had another one about developing success from failure, which Rory Smartwart said was just loser talk.

Romulus shook his head, his snake hair sighing. 'Well, believe in Vulcan's might, then. His army stretches the breadth of Romana and each day it grows stronger. Now come, eat. You must build your strength for what lies ahead.'

I shrugged, trying to ignore the smell of fresh pastries wafting from the tent. But my stomach wasn't playing ball. I was so hungry I'd have even eaten some of Mrs Burden's lamb fries. And if you don't know what lamb fries are, look them up – yep, I was that hungry! Plus Romulus was right. Whatever I decided to do, I needed to keep my strength up. I followed – my, erg, gorgon brother – towards the tent.

'Hurry up, you two!' shouted Felix, popping his head out of the gap between the door flaps. 'Last one inside is a **Gaul**!'

CHAPTER 18

THE OWL OF MINERVA

'**H**i-de-hoot-hoot!'

'What?' I shot up.

I must have fallen asleep on the dining couch while I was waiting for Romulus and Remus to get back. They'd been called away, Felix dropping his fourth slice of honey cake on the fancy tapestry rug and charging out of the tent behind them. Leaving me alone with the cake – which I wasn't going to complain about.

'Hi-de-hoot-hoot!"

What was that noise? I rubbed my eyes, head fuzzy, stomach swollen from too much honey cake.

'I said, hello!'

A sphere of white light was hovering above the couch. It flashed and smoke filled the tent. Through the haze I saw an owl. A tiny owl with a slightly wonky beak.

'Charming!' The owl flapped its brown and white speckled wings and landed on the table next to the fruit bowl. 'I'll have you know I'm in the top quartile for my breed, actually. As for the wonky beak comment, well, I'll let it go on this occasion.'

It's just a dream, Livi. Just a dream—

'Not quite, chick.' The owl stood up straight. 'More an apparition. A divine apparition, to be precise. Now shush, we don't have much time.'

What? This was weird even by dream standards. I mean, not only was the little owl talking, but she was reading my thoughts!

'Not so much reading them, chick, as hearing them. Reading suggests I'm trying to get inside your head. I don't have to try. I've never had to try at anything. What with my extreme wisdomnous, and all.'

Groaning, I pulled a cushion over my head. I knew I shouldn't have eaten all that cake. Too much sugar before bed always gives me nightmares.

'How many times do I have to tell you, this is not a dream.' The cushion dented with the weight of the owl, who started to peck my fingers. 'Now come on. We've work to do.'

I threw the cushion down. I mean, what did this dream-owl want from me?

The owl huffed and jumped on to the back of the couch. 'This isn't about what I want, chick. It's about what you want. I'm here to guide you. To help you decide. The name's Athene. Athene Noctua.'

'The Owl of Minerva? Can you ask the wisdom goddess where my dad is?'

'And why would I want to do that? I'm the one with all the wisdomnous. She might have taken the credit but those we mentored know the truth.'

Whatever. Sounds like someone had a bad case of the jealous legs.

'Jealous of *her*? She's a total fraud. It is my wisdomnous that abides. And it is me, here now, offering you guidance while she sits in her hot tub drinking **nectar**.'

'Sorry.' Maybe I had been a bit rude, but how was I to know the owl was going to read my thoughts. 'So, can you tell me how to find Dad, then?'

'Nice try, chick, but how exactly is that guiding you? Did Ulysses expect me to give him the world on a plate? No, he knew a hero has to take action.' The owl folded her wings across her chest. 'He's another one she took the credit for. Though she was at least grateful back then. Treated me well enough at first but then she started to get all uppity. Liked the sound of her own voice—'

That'd make two of them then. I shut my eyes

and stuck my fingers in my ears. The owl was doing my head in—

'Doing your head in! Silvia Fortuna Juno De Luca, what bit of this don't you get? You are the Undecided, and you are going to need all the help you can get!'

The Undecided – why did people keep calling me that—

'That's what everyone calls you here. The Undecided – the first mortal child born to the gods since the founding of Romana.'

'Stop doing that.'

'What?'

'Getting inside my head.'

'But it's just so empty. And my wisdomnous is so huge. Now shush and I'll explain all! Let's start with the sybil and the prophecy—'

Not the prophecy thing again.

'I said shush!'

Standing up straight, Athene Noctua began to sing:

'*Romana, Romana, born of forge and fire,*

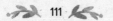

111

Romana, Romana, the empire's funeral pyre.
Jupiter, Jupiter a golden arrow did bestow,
Upon Vulcan, the mighty Vulcan—'

'STOP!' I thought Felix's singing was bad, but this took things to a whole new eardrum-shrivelling level. No wonder owls weren't invited to join the dawn chorus. 'Do you have to sing it?!'

'There she goes again with the charm offensive.' Eyes round like chariot wheels, Athene Noctua hooted and flapped her wings. 'Now just quit with the negativity, will you. I haven't got to the important bit yet—'

'Hello?'

Athene Noctua twisted her neck 180 degrees, so her head was facing the doorway. 'Oh feathers, look what you've done now with all your talking. We're out of time.' She shuffled along the back of the couch until she was right by my head. 'Your brothers must not know I came to you. Because if they know, there's a chance *she* will find out too. And I really can't be doing with one of Bellona's tantrums. In fact, I can't be doing with any of this.

But needs must. Some things are bigger than our own wants and hoots. The sooner you realize that the better.'

Erg, OK. Remind me NEVER to eat sugar again, will you? Well at least not before bedtime.

'Silvia!' called Remus. 'We're back!'

Athene Noctua looked down her wonky beak at me. 'I'll return as soon as I can. Meanwhile, keep your mortal mouth shut about this and try not to do anything stupid.'

CHAPTER 19

ROMULUS, REMUS AND THE CYCLOPS

Heart pounding, I sat up. The tent felt smaller somehow, the air hot and dense.

'Silvia, is everything OK?'

Remus.

I rubbed my eyes. I wasn't sure where my dream had ended and this conversation had begun.

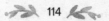

Maybe I was still dreaming? Maybe none of this was real?

I didn't have time to think about it for too long, though, because there was a gurgling sound and something that looked a bit like a supercharged Baby Yoda darted through the tent doors towards me. It grabbed hold of my leg and started to suck my knee.

'Poly,' scolded Romulus, following the Baby Yoda thing into the tent. 'I thought I told you to wait.' He shook his head and peeled the green tot from my leg. 'Sorry, Silvia, she's been pillaging the beehives again. Honey always makes her a bit wild.'

Oh my Greco-Roman gods, Poly was adorable. Who knew having a giant eye stuck in the middle of your forehead could be such a good look?

'Mama,' she cried. 'Mama!'

'No, Poly,' laughed Remus. 'This is our sister, Silvia. Say hello now.'

'Mama,' said the baby cyclops, sticking her finger up her nose. 'Mama!'

'There's no getting through to her,' said Romulus sadly. 'We keep telling her who mother is, but she hasn't really settled. I think she misses home.'

'Bellona took her away from her home?'

'She'll be OK,' shrugged Remus unconvincingly. 'It took all of us time to adjust.'

Adjust? I hadn't thought about the fact the twins might have been brought here too. Did Bellona abandon all her children? Was that just what she did? Then force them to come and live with her? Was that what she was expecting me to do too? Erg, I don't think so.

Romulus sighed and shook his head. 'Come now, Silvia. It's time to meet your horse.'

A horse – I was getting my own horse?! I'd always wanted a pony, but we could never afford one. I did have a riding lesson once when Dad won first prize in the school raffle. The instructor said I was a natural, which was a surprise to me too because I'm decidedly average at most things. Except cross-country and French – I'm totally rubbish at them! Anyway, stop distracting me. We need to focus on the positive – the horse could just be my ticket out of here.

Outside in the parade area, a group of legionaries practised their drills with wooden swords while long-limbed auxiliaries threw javelins at a makeshift dummy. I could feel their eyes following me. Nosy nanas, or what!

'Mama,' said Poly, grabbing my hand. 'Mama swing.'

'She likes you,' said Romulus, taking hold of Poly's other hand. 'After three, now!'

Together we swung the squealing baby cyclops high into the air.

'Again again,' she said.

Smiling, I tightened my grip on Poly's scaly hand, my swing perfectly in time with Romulus's as we stomped across the parched grass. She really was the sweetest little thing. It was a shame I didn't have time to get to know her better. But I had to get to Dad. I had to find a way to fix this. One that didn't involve taking baby cyclops from their homes or stealing arrows from dragons.

'Why would Bellona bring a baby here?'

'She's forty-seven, actually. Mother said maturing slowly was a poor excuse not to join the cause. Poly must play her part like everybody else.'

'And what is her part, exactly?'

'To stand beside you, sister,' said Remus. 'That is the part we must all play, if peace is to prevail over tyranny.'

'Erg, thanks, but I think you're mixing me up with somebody else.'

'There is no mistake.' Romulus's hair curled upwards, the snakes staring at me intently. 'It is written in the prophecy. Only the Undecided can end this conflict.'

End this? I couldn't even stand up to Rory Smartwart, let alone take on a bunch of lava soldiers in a battle no one had even bothered to explain to me.

'Mama!' Poly let go of my hand. She bent down and clawed at the soil with her long fingernails. 'Mama wiggle!'

Eww, was that a worm she was waving? Yep, and

it was a big one too. She waved it again, proudly, before licking the dirt off and sucking it into her mouth like a piece of spaghetti.

'No, Poly!' said Romulus, scraping the worm out of her mouth. 'Go and find Felix for me, there's a good girl. He was supposed to be collecting Silvia's kit.'

I chewed my lip, forehead crinkling. The busy camp was no place for a baby to wander. Especially the parade area.

'Oh, don't worry,' said Remus. 'She has a nose like a hunting dog. She'll soon sniff Felix out.' He dug a wooden training sword out of a large clay urn and threw it at me. 'Meanwhile, how about you show me what you're made of. Mother said you're quite the swordsmith, though, of course, it is with a bow and arrow you really shine. Just as the prophecy foretold.'

'And how would she know?' I caught the **rudis**, more through reflex than anything. It felt heavier than the fake LARP swords I practised with at home. I raised it in front of me, testing the weight.

'Oh, she knows more than you realize,' Romulus said. 'None of this is an accident.'

A shiver ran down my spine. I knew Bellona had somehow brought us here for a reason but the idea of her watching me from a distance was just so totally wrong. I was more determined than ever to leave.

'Sorry, I don't really feel like sparring,' I said. 'Can't we just go and get my horse?'

'Of course,' said Romulus. 'Remus, **subsisto**! You know time is of the essence.'

'Oh, don't be such a spoilsport.' Remus smiled, the snakes sticking out their tongues as though to mock me. 'Are you scared of losing or something?' Dancing on his toes, he lunged at me.

I blocked his attack and lunged right back, jabbing him in the stomach. 'Too easy.'

'But I wasn't ready.' Remus's hair drooped, the snake heads hanging limply around his shoulders.

'You never are,' laughed Romulus.

Remus stuck his grey tongue out. 'I'll take you down, any day.' He pinged his goggles. 'And those lava soldiers!'

'As you like it, brother.' Romulus folded his arms. 'Mother already told you. Our special talents are useless against the lava soldiers. That is why Silvia must retrieve the arrow this evening. Before Vulcan's forces can grow any stronger.'

Talk about guilt trip. 'If the arrow is so important, why doesn't Bellona go and fetch it herself?'

'Because you're the one chosen by the Fates,' Remus replied. 'The first mortal child born to the founding gods. Your destiny is forewritten—'

'What, by some silly prophecy? Nobody believes in that sort of stuff any more.'

'Maybe not in Britannia,' said Romulus. 'But here the Fates determine our destiny. And like it or not, your destiny is one with Romana's. Now come, let's go and get your horse.'

CHAPTER 20

MEETING TITUS

The horses were at the far end of the interval-lum, near the brook. We continued past the red-faced legionaries practising their formations and made our way towards the makeshift paddock, waving at Poly and Felix, who were sitting under a clump of chestnut trees making daisy chains.

'Mama!' cried Poly, charging towards us. 'Mama!'

'**Caute!**' Romulus's snake hair grimaced as Poly ran right through the legs of a powerful white horse. 'You know better than to upset Titus.'

'Horsey,' said Poly, stopping suddenly to pick up a dead frog that had been baked hard as leather by the sun. 'Horsey, Mama.'

'Clever girl,' said Romulus. 'Yes, the stallion belongs to Mama. Now, put the frog down.'

'Mama!' Poly blew a snot bubble and threw the frog at Felix. 'Froggy, Mama.' Giggling, she ran off towards the brook, Felix trailing after her shouting something about poo and pine cones and the glory of Romana. I turned to the stallion.

'I wouldn't get too close,' said Romulus. 'He has a temper as fierce as Bellona's.'

The stallion whinnied indignantly.

'He's magnificent.'

'He was a present from Mother's latest suitor,' said Remus. 'Found him wandering around outside the camp. Should have left him there too, if you ask me.'

'Aww, don't be mean,' I said. 'Horses have feelings too.'

Ears pinned, the stallion watched me curiously. He was tethered to a wooden cart, the dappled sun reflecting off his pure white coat, giving it a majestic golden glow.

'Careful, sister!' Romulus's snake hair was throwing a right hissy. What was the problem? The horse wanted me to go to him. I just knew he did.

'It's fine,' I said, edging forward. 'You don't mind me saying hello, do you, fella?'

The stallion's ear twitched. I decided to take this as a good sign. 'Here,' I said, picking up his water bucket and plonking it down in front of him. 'There you go.'

Titus whinnied softly. His tail shining in the sunlight, he began to drink. Slowly, I reached over and touched his neck. He whinnied again and nuzzled my shoulder.

'Well, blow me down with a phoenix feather,' said Remus. 'I'd have bet my own twin brother on you taking a kick.'

The thought had passed my mind too. Titus was wound so tightly he could snap any minute.

But, somehow, I knew he wouldn't hurt me. That he was drawn to me just as much as I was to him. I climbed on to the cart.

'No, Silv—'

It must have been quite a look I gave Romulus, because he stopped mid-sentence, the snakes tracking my every move.

'Here, Titus,' I said, my voice kind but firm. 'That a boy.'

Titus stepped closer towards the cart. I placed my hand on his neck and he eased in towards me, waiting patiently as I climbed clumsily into the saddle and undid the rope attached to his halter. 'Good boy,' I said, scratching between his ears. 'Good boy.'

Romulus smiled and the snakes grew still. 'So, the Undecided is a horse whisperer.'

Apparently so! Amazing, hey?! Little old me, a horsey prodigy. Who'd have thought it?

'Steady,' I said, pulling gently on the reins and squeezing Titus with my legs to encourage him to go forward. 'Steady.'

Titus pulled away from the cart and eased into a trot. It felt weird riding without stirrups, but not as weird as having gorgons for brothers, so I decided to go with it.

'Good boy,' I said, trying not to think too much about what I was doing and allowing myself to sink into his rhythm. 'Shall we go a little faster?'

Titus broke into a canter. Wow! It seemed I really was a natural. Which was a good job, given what happened next.

'Careful, Poly!' I called as she charged towards us. I heaved on Titus's reins. Clumps of earth flying into the air, he made a sudden stop, throwing me forward in the saddle.

'Uh-oh,' said Poly, looking like she was about to burst into tears.

'It's OK, Poly,' I said, steadying myself. 'I'm fine.'

'No OK,' said Poly, pointing at the turquoise blur flying towards us. 'Mama, uh-oh.'

CHAPTER 21

TWENTY SACKS OF GOLD AND A BARREL OF FLAMINGO TONGUES

Mama, uh-oh indeed! Legionaries scattered as Bellona's chariot thundered towards the ground, almost taking the slowest soldier's head off. The dummy he was using for spear practice wasn't so lucky – its pumpkin head flew towards me like a football.

'Mmm,' said Bellona, climbing out of the chariot. 'Might have known you two grumps would form an alliance.' She ran her hand over Titus's shoulder, and he blew out through his nostrils. 'Still, I'm glad he came round – would have been a shame to stew such a fine stallion.'

Titus snorted and pawed the ground.

'Naughty, Mama!' said Poly. 'Horsey nice.'

Bellona rolled her eyes. 'Isn't it time for your nap, Poly?'

'Mama poo-poop!' Poly stuck her green tongue out and ran off towards the brook again.

Bellona shook her head. She pointed her spear at me. 'And why isn't she kitted up!' What was her problem? She was looking at me like I'd just thrown up in her lap. 'I specifically told you boys to get Silvia mission-ready.'

'Sorry, mother,' said Romulus. 'We were just checking out her horsemanship.'

'It's her talent,' said Felix. 'It has to be! Want to know what mine is, Silvia?'

'Not now, Felix!' raged Bellona. She waved her

spear at the twins. 'I've told you boys before; I want action, not excuses. Do I have to remind you of the repercussions if she fails?'

'Erg, I am here, you know!' They were talking about me like I was invisible or something.

Maybe I was invisible, because Bellona completely ignored me again and continued to lay into Romulus and Remus. 'Let me down again and I'll court-martial the pair of you.'

Remus's snake hair curled into tight spirals. It made him look younger, somehow – Year 10, max.

'Please don't be angry, Mamma,' said Felix. 'It's all my fault—'

Bellona held her arm out, palm centimetres from Felix's nose. 'Talk to the hand, Felix. Talk to the hand.' She rummaged in her chariot and handed him a large glass jar with something squirmy inside. 'Here, take this with you.'

'Scylla!' Felix tapped the jar. 'Welcome, sister!'

The creature inside the jar bared its teeth – all six sets of them – and thrashed against the glass. Somehow, I didn't think I'd ever be doing cuddle night with Scylla.

Cuddle night – a wave of sadness hit me like a minotaur. What I wouldn't do to be cuddled up with Dad, right now. If only I'd gone downstairs and watched those DVDs with him, none of this would have happened.

'Take good care of her now,' continued Bellona. 'I had a terrible time getting her into the jar. She's as vicious as her namesake and just as sneaky. She'll make a brilliant addition to the team.'

'To the team?'

'Yes,' said Bellona. 'Team Annihilate Vulcan! Families that slay together stay together.'

'Erg, OK. Nice pep talk, but annihilation and slaying aren't really my thing.'

'And what *is* your thing?'

'I don't know. Baking Vulcan a cake and asking nicely if he'll give me my dad back? Romulus said the arrow would bring peace.'

'Peace and stability are a matter of perspective. Now, stop being such a know-it-all and do as you are told. I really don't know what all the fuss is about. It's not like I'm sending you on some great odyssey. The arrow lies little more than an hour away.'

'What about the dragon and the lava soldiers?'

'Dragons, actually,' said Bellona. 'Vulcan is rather fond of them. The metal ones he crafted to guard the perimeters of his territory are particularly ferocious. But you'll find a way through. It is your destiny.'

'Reassuring. Not!' And I didn't want to have to find a way through. 'Why can't you just talk to him? Offer some sort of olive branch or something? Isn't that what you people do—'

'Seriously, Silvia, I've been talking to Vulcan for over two thousand years! I'm sick of talking. This whole Romana thing was a terrible mistake.'

'Romana thing?' But Bellona wasn't stopping for questions.

'I thought we could have some fun together, what with most of the other gods going into retirement, but I'd forgotten how infuriating he was with his silly little hammer and unsightly beard.'

'A beard is hardly a reason to annihilate someone—'

'By Jupiter himself, you are almost as insufferable as your uncle! Do you want to save your father or not? Because time is running out for our Ben.' Bellona ran her finger over the tip of her spear. 'Such a sweet soul, and handy with a **gladius** too. I still have a soft spot for him.'

'Are you for real?'

'Oh, don't look at me like that, Silvia.' Bellona shook her head defiantly. 'Vulcan started this. I'm just trying to do what's best for Romana. Now, enough! Here's your brother with an update.'

Hooves thundered on parched earth, dust forming an angry grey cloud along the road.

'Tiber!' called Felix. 'Hooray!'

A centaur? The same centaur who was on my TV no less! Well, I guess we had a sea monster, gorgons and a cyclops in the family, why not throw in a centaur for good measure? Seriously, he was awesome. It was like someone had sliced him in half at the waist and plonked him on to a horse's shoulders. A powerful chestnut horse with a gleaming coat and chocolate-brown tail.

'Yo, fam,' he said, fist-bumping Felix. 'What's going down?'

Bellona rolled her eyes. 'I was rather hoping you'd tell us, given you're the scout. Now say hello to your sisters – Scylla and Silvia.'

The glass beads on his necklace glistening, Tiber pushed his surfer-dude hair behind his ears and tapped Scylla's jar. She thrashed against the glass, an angry squirming mass of tentacles and teeth. 'Sick!' he said, turning towards me. 'So that must make you the Undecided. What's up, sis?'

I reached to take Tiber's outstretched hand, but he pulled it away suddenly. 'Gotcha,' he said, pressing his thumb to his nose and wiggling his fingers.

Wow, the last time I'd seen someone pull that trick he was wearing a red plastic nose and standing in a circus ring. He wasn't funny either.

Tiber poked Felix in the stomach. 'Got to have a laugh, haven't you, bro! Hey, why did the horseman wear a peacock on his head?'

'I don't know,' said Felix.

'Because he wanted to be the *centaur* of attention!'

Bellona's eyes blazed turquoise. 'Enough of this horseplay! What did you uncover?'

The centaur unbuckled his crammed leather satchel and pulled out a wad of papyrus sheets. 'Dude, you're not gonna like it, but these things are everywhere—'

'How many times must I tell you? Do not call me dude.' Bellona tore a bunch of papyri from Tiber's hand. She held one up for me to examine. 'Still want to reason with Vulcan?'

I took the papyrus from Bellona and studied the picture – the picture of me. Like, what! No way were my teeth that wonky.

Or maybe they were . . . ? Brilliant, something else for Rory Smartwart to have a go about! And yes, I know my teeth and Rory Smartwart were strange things to focus on given the circumstances, but the circumstances were just too scary to contemplate. Vulcan had only gone and put a price on my head!

'Leaning over my shoulder, Remus let out a long, slow whistle. 'Wow! Twenty sacks of gold and a barrel of flamingo tongues? That's one serious reward.'

'Flamingo tongues?' I said, once again choosing to focus on the irrelevant. 'Why would anyone want a barrel of flamingo tongues?'

'They're a delicacy,' said Romulus. He pinched his fingers and thumb together and kissed them flamboyantly. 'Beautiful sauteed with **silphium**.' He leant in towards the wanted poster, his brow furrowing. 'Strange, only—'

'I'll take that,' said Bellona, snatching the papyrus. 'Evidence of Vulcan's war crimes.' She studied the poster for a moment, her blood-red aura crackling and popping as she muttered something about incompetence and floggings. 'Please tell me you retrieved them all, Tiber.'

'Mostly, but I had to abort the mission to go and get my hooves reshod. Won't make any difference anyway. The whole of Romana is talking about the price on the Undecided's head. Word is she'll be dead by morning.'

'Then we must bite the sling-bullet now,' said Bellona. 'She'll leave at dusk.'

Romulus's hair hissed, the snakes standing upright. 'But it's too dangerous. We have to take her back to Britannia and seal the gateway. Now is not the time for rash decisions.'

'Erg, hello!' They were doing it again. Talking about me like I wasn't there.

Bellona raised her spear. 'The prophecy is clear – the Undecided will find a way to make the arrow hers.'

'Can't she drink the nectar?'

'No, Felix, she can't!' Bellona gave Felix a look that would make an ordinary kid come out in boils. 'Which bit of "Undecided" aren't you getting?'

'But I want to know for sure what her talent is—'

'Felix, I'm telling you, zip it! Off you go, on the double! One more word and I'll send you to the Underworld to visit your Great Uncle Orcus. I hear he's looking for an apprentice.'

Felix bit his lip. Staring at me sadly, he started to

make his way back across the forum.

'Mamma-dude,' smiled Tiber. 'Of course, you know best. But that's a lot of dough, and you know what they say, there's no loyalty when it comes to gold and flamingo tongues. Maybe it wouldn't hurt for Silvia to at least lay low for a while.'

'Enough!' Bellona's aura flickered scarlet, a wave of heat forcing Tiber backwards. 'She leaves tonight, under the cover of darkness. Do not question me again. Last time I checked, it was me who was the war goddess!'

Blood thundered in my ears. I was sick of them ignoring me. Telling me what I was or wasn't going to do. Making out I had no choice in any of this. And worst of all, they seemed to have forgotten why I was actually there.

'What about Dad? What happens to him if I just go home?'

'Then he is doomed,' said Bellona. 'We all are.'

Doomed. That sounded kind of serious.

'Tell me what I need to do.'

CHAPTER 22

TOILET TALK

Wow, I thought my quarters were fancy, but Bellona's tent took glamping to a whole new level. What was with all the statues? It looked like Narcissus wasn't the only one who liked to look at himself. As for the feast that had been laid out on low marble tables, it could have fed a small country; so long as that country didn't mind eating stuffed dormice and cured lamb brains. Next best thing to flamingo tongues, apparently.

Not that I could have eaten anything right then. Not with the worry worms churning in my stomach. You see, I may have agreed to fetch the arrow, but that didn't mean I was happy about it. Everything was happening so quickly. I'd barely had time to change out of my trackie bottoms and fetch my kit from the weapon store and off I was about to pop.

Bellona, on the other hand, seemed a little too happy about it all. This party thing, for a start. Romana was on the brink of war – a war against her own brother no less – and she wanted to have a big family do! She'd even had us dress in the same ceremonial gold tunics, so we'd look good on the new mosaic she'd commissioned to mark the occasion. Seriously, we looked like a bunch of Christmas crackers—

'Are you OK, Silvia?'

'Yes.' I nodded. It was what Romulus wanted to hear.

'Are you sure?' said Remus.

I shifted in my seat. The way the snakes were staring at me was making me really uncomfortable.

Romulus shuffled up the couch towards me. 'I've been reflecting,' he said. 'Mother is right, there is no going back. The thread of your destiny has been woven.' He waved to Felix, who was near the entrance trying to catch the kamikaze moths that were flinging themselves at the giant bronze oil lamps. 'I wish things were different, but the die has been cast. It is you who must restore peace to Romana.'

The worry worms squirmed. There was so much depending on me but despite Romulus's assurances my gut was in total conflict with my heart. 'Where's the loo?'

'Pardon?'

'You know, the toilet.'

'She means the latrina,' said Tiber. He was wearing a new set of amber beads and his tail had been threaded with gold ribbon.

Remus raised his eyebrows. 'Well, why didn't you just say that? Use the conveniences in Bellona's personal chambers. Though good luck finding the **tersorium**. Poly was using it as a teething stick earlier.'

'Hi-de-hoot-hoot!'

The free-standing oil lamp flickered, shadows dancing across the pitched roof of the tent.

'I said, hi-de-hoot-hoot!'

What? The little owl from my dreams again? How is that even possible? Have I fallen asleep on the toilet?

'No, of course not, you numpty,' Athene Noctua said, landing on top of the carved wooden screen that sectioned off the toilet area from Bellona's elaborate bedchambers. 'But your measly mortal mind had wandered. Now is not the time for daydreaming, Silvia.'

Like she can talk about timing. I was on the bog, for Jupiter's sake!

'Oh, get over yourself. I've never understood this newfangled hang-up with toilet privacy. We all do it!'

Brilliant, like it isn't bad enough she's talking to me when I'm on the bog, she's reading my every thought again! What does she think she's doing?

'I'm doing what I've done for centuries, chick. I'm sharing my extreme wisdomnous. The question is, what in the name of Romana do you think you're doing? Which bit of "don't do anything stupid" didn't you understand?' Athene Noctua flapped her wings and landed on the arm of the distinctly un-Roman bronze commode.

I shooed her away. 'Can you at least let me pull my knickers up before you lecture me?'

'Fine!' Athene Noctua did the twisty neck thing again, so her head was facing the wall of the tent. 'Now, let's get down to business . . . if you'll pardon the pun.'

Hilarious. I do not have time for this.

'Maybe if you'd taken a little more time to think you wouldn't be in such a pickle. So, what are we going to do—'

'I'm not in a pickle. And I don't know what you're going to do but I'm going to get the arrow.'

What else can I do? Vulcan has put a price on my head. I have no choice but to stand with Bellona—

'OK, chick,' said Athene Noctua, following me over to the washstand where I poured water into the fluted bronze bowl. 'If you're sure . . . only you don't seem very sure, what with the worry worms kicking off again.' She pointed at my stomach like I didn't know where the bad feeling was sitting. 'And this reward business – well, it really doesn't sound like the Vulcan I remember.'

'Remember? Have you not seen his army of lava soldiers?'

'Of course I've seen them. I see everything. And I've seen enough to know things aren't always what they seem. Ask the Trojans – now there's a lesson in not taking things at face value.' The owl's wide amber eyes stared deep into mine. It was proper weird. Like she was searching for something. 'There's nothing weird about searching for the truth, chick.' She shook her head sadly. 'Maybe you should try it sometime.'

'But I've seen the posters for myself. My dad and

all those missing people forced to join his lava army. Vulcan has to be stopped.'

'You still don't get it, do you? There's more than one version of the truth. Get with the programme! The Undecided can either bring together or divide.'

'Like I have a choice in any of this. All I want is to get my dad back.'

'Of course you have a choice. Your fate is one with Romana's, but your path is still to be decided.'

'What's that supposed to mean?'

'The clue's in the name, chick. There's more than one way to bake a cake. This way, you're going to get your fingers burnt.'

'Stop talking in riddles because you think it's clever. If you've got something to say, just say it.'

'I told you before – I can't tell you what to do. That's not how these things work. But what I will say is, ex nihilo nihil fit.'

Nothing comes from nothing. 'Thanks for that. Everything's much clearer now.'

There was a drum roll and the low hum of

chatter in the main tent fell silent.

'I have to go,' I said.

'That you do. We don't want her to come look-ing for you. She'll pluck me as soon as look at me and Jupiter knows what she'd do to you.' Feathers standing on edge, Athene Noctua began to glow again. 'Good luck now, Silvia. Such a great weight on your mortal shoulders, but believe me when I tell you, the answers are there for the taking. Find your wisdomnous, please. For all our sakes!'

CHAPTER 23

THE DECIDED

Bellona's chariot had been wheeled into position in front of the couches, her ceremonial cape draped around it like a river of gold, almost covering the giant Persian rug. Ignoring the fact she was giving me the evils, I squoze into the gap between Felix and Romulus.

Poly gurgled excitedly at me from her perch on

Remus's knee. 'Mama,' she cried, pointing at the oiled musicians peeking out from behind the tapestry curtain divider. 'Mama!'

'Ahem!' Bellona lifted her curved bronze trumpet and blew . . .

and blew . . .

and blew.

I'm telling you, there were ships on the Tyne turning round, right now.

'Make it stop!' mouthed Tiber with his fingers in his ears. 'Please make it stop.'

But Bellona continued to blow the trumpet for what felt like an eternity. Maybe I was immortal after all?

'Thank you, children,' she finally said, her cheeks taking a few seconds to deflate. Composing her smile, she passed the trumpet to a glossy-haired guard with teeth so white he could have been in a toothpaste advert. Oh my Greco-Roman gods, it was the soldier from the forum. I'd recognize those gnashers anywhere.

'Cornelius Lucius Sulla,' whispered Romulus,

confirming my suspicions. 'Praetorian Prefect and Mother's latest suitor.'

'Total snipe eel,' said Remus. 'Always telling tales to mother. The soldiers call him Potty-Mouth.'

'Potty-Mouth?'

'Yes, because he whitens his teeth with wee.'

Ugh. The communal bum-wiper was bad enough, but this took things to a whole new level.

'Extreme, hey?' said Tiber. 'I thought the mortals had stopped doing that!'

'When you're quite finished, Tiber!' Wow, Bellona sounded like my head teacher. She'd be dishing out detentions next! 'So,' she continued, 'the whole family together at last, ready to taste the glorious thrill of war! Jupiter knows, I haven't felt this proud since I led Trajan to victory in Dacia. And with the sacred arrow finally in my grasp, victory will be mine again as we put Vulcan's fire out once and for all.'

That nagging feeling again. There was nothing glorious about war. I got that Vulcan had to be stopped, but I thought the point of me fetching the arrow was to bring about peace?

Remus winced as Poly tugged yet again at his snake hair. He set her down on the floor and pulled the tray of stuffed dormice towards her.

'Mama!' she cried, making a grab for the biggest roasted rodent on the platter, and swallowing it whole.

'Good girl, Poly,' said Bellona. 'Let us feast and enjoy each other's company, for there is much to celebrate!'

There she goes again. Celebrate? In a few hours' time, I could be dragon fodder and Romana plunged into civil war. Maybe Athene Noctua was right. Maybe I had rushed into this.

'Silvia, are you sure you're OK?' A hundred glassy eyes stared at me in concern.

'Yes, well, it's just . . .' I turned my gaze from Romulus to Bellona. 'Are you sure we're doing the right thing?'

'Of course,' said Remus. 'It's just last-minute jitters. You are the Undecided, after all. You're destined to dither.'

'Nice!' said Tiber, fist-bumping Remus. 'Who said gorgons have no sense of humour?'

I smiled. Maybe there was something in this prophecy thing. I was never much good at making decisions. Most days, I couldn't even decide what socks to wear.

I looked at Romulus, who nodded reassuringly. 'Vulcan must be stopped. We stand with you, Silvia—'

'Band!' Bellona bellowed. She clapped her hands together, tapping her foot impatiently. 'Where is the band?'

There was a groan and a bang from behind the curtain divider. Bowing apologetically, the group of flustered musicians appeared and began to set up their instruments.

'Oh no, not the Lyres,' said Remus. 'Let's just hope Mother doesn't decide to sing.'

'Mama,' said Poly, chewing on a dormouse tail like it was a liquorice lace. 'Mama, yum!'

'Bad luck, bro!' Tiber thumped Remus on the shoulder as Bellona counted the musicians in. 'The

Virgil Waltz, your favourite!'

Remus grimaced. 'I knew I should have volunteered to guard the perimeters from flamingo tongue-loving mercenaries.'

I sighed.

Romulus's snake hair drooped. 'Remus, that was in bad taste. Ignore him, Silvia. I am afraid it is the gorgon way to laugh in the face of adversity.'

'It's fine,' I said. And I meant it. It was Dad's way too. Laughter and LARPing were how we got through. He'd like my new brothers. I just knew he would.

I glanced over at Bellona. She clearly wasn't one to sit around worrying either. Not judging by the way she was twirling Potty-Mouth around on the makeshift dance floor.

'Go, Mamma-dude!' cried Tiber, trotting on the spot like he was doing dressage. 'Go!'

Pushing Potty-Mouth out of the way, Bellona lifted her skirt tail. Winking at Tiber, she traversed the rug in a move that was somehow a cross between a funeral march and the moonwalk.

'Yeah, baby!' Tiber bent his front legs and lifted Poly on to one of the couches. Taking Felix's hand, he helped him climb up beside her. 'Come on, little dudes. Let's see what you've got!'

Hilarious! Even Bellona couldn't resist laughing at Poly's cute wiggle.

Remus shrugged and pushed Scylla's jar further away from the edge of the table it was sitting on. The sea monster continued to sway to the music. 'Welcome to the family, Silvia,' he laughed. 'You don't have to be able to jiggle wiggle, but it helps.'

I laughed too, pushing away the doubt. Fetching the arrow was the right thing to do. Not just for Dad but for my brothers and sisters too. If Vulcan could put a price on my head, then he could do the same to Felix or Poly. And what about all the innocent Romanans that had been going missing? No one was safe unless I put an end to this.

CHAPTER 24

DEPARTURE

It was time. A jewelled sword and dagger sitting heavy on my hip, I followed Romulus out of Bellona's quarters and into the humid night. A storm was beginning to build, the low cloud trapping the heat and making it feel like the sky was closing in. Hooking the elaborately decorated bow I'd been issued over my shoulder, I glanced towards the horizon where the orange sky glowed like radioactive marmalade.

'He grows stronger by the hour,' said Romulus.

'On the plus side, at least I won't have a problem finding the cave.'

Romulus's snake hair chuckled nervously. We'd gone through the drill at least a dozen times that afternoon. The dragon's lair was less than an hour away, at Grotta Azzurra, a remote sea cave just beyond the wall of lava soldiers below the volcanic plateaux of Solfatara. A remote sea cave only accessible by a narrow uneven causeway. A narrow uneven causeway that was sometimes underwater, sometimes not, but always under the watchful eye of the **Nereids** – who are, apparently, quite friendly for sea nymphs, unless they think you're about to nick the sacred arrow.

'Focus on one problem at a time,' was Bellona's advice when I pointed out the odds weren't exactly in my favour. 'Stick to the drill and remember, you were born for this.'

Reassuring. Not.

Darting back into the lines of tents to avoid the rowdy legionnaires playing **Tali** at the edge of the parade, I followed Romulus towards the intervallum where Remus was waiting with Titus. Bellona had instructed that my departure should be secret. There would be no ceremony or military salute to send me on my way. Not with the price on my head. Instead, I was to slip out of the camp quietly via the service hatch cut into the high boundary fence.

Titus whinnied, his coat glistening in the strange orange light.

'Good boy,' I whispered, taking his reins.

'Here, sister,' said Remus, bending down and cupping his hands together to give me a leg-up. 'Everything is as we agreed. May Mercury's speed be with you!'

'Thank you,' I said, pulling down my tunic and reaching for Titus's saddle. Not my most sophisticated of mountings but the stallion didn't seem to mind my clumsiness. In fact, I really don't know what Romulus was worrying about when he suggested I choose an *easier* horse. Not that I chose Titus. We chose each other.

'Calm, boy.' I pulled on Titus's reins as he threw his head back, his nostrils flaring. 'What is it?'

A dark shadow fell. Remus drew his sword.

'Easy, Titus!' Raising my knees, I leant forward in the saddle to steady myself. Again, somehow, I just seemed to know what to do. 'Wait!'

And then I saw it.

The monstrous raptor that made your average albatross look like a canary . . . the monstrous raptor with the body, tail and back legs of a lion! Hovering right above us!

'Griffin!' cried Romulus.

The twins had warned me about the fierce griffins who lived in the no man's land between the camp and Vulcan's army. Bellona tolerated them because she enjoyed hunting them, even if her sport did mean losing the odd legionary. Seriously, how was I related to this woman?

'Go, Silvia, I'll deal with this!' Romulus tugged at his goggles but then paused. 'And whatever you do, don't look back!'

The griffin swooped. Screeching, it dive-bombed us, its breath so foul it burnt my nostrils. Remus threw his sword at the creature, Romulus meanwhile taking his goggles off and chucking them on the floor. Time to look away.

I pulled on Titus's reins. 'Leg it!'

Titus didn't need to be asked twice. He took off like a cheetah that had just been bitten on the bum by a hyena. I tried to steer him towards the service hatch, but he continued to charge towards the boundary fence . . . the very high, very spiky boundary fence we had no chance of clearing. *Mmm, maybe I'm not such a natural horseman after all.*

But now wasn't the time for doubt.

The griffin's hot breath scorching my neck, I heaved on Titus's reins, trying to turn him. This would have been a very good time for Romulus or Remus to do the starey stone thing! I could hear Romulus goading the bird behind me, but it would seem the griffin only had eyes for me. Its finger-like talons were just centimetres from my neck, its blood-curdling screeches echoing around the camp.

And now there were guards screeching at me too. Swords drawn, spears raised, they called out from the watchtower: 'Stop!'

But I couldn't stop.

Not now.

It wasn't just that Titus had gone rogue, there was too much at stake.

Too much to fight for.

I had to take my chance.

Believe.

Because if Titus believed we could do this, then I could believe too.

The watchmen beat their shields with their swords, and the griffin finally paused.

'Go, Silvia,' called Remus. 'The Undecided will find a way.'

Easy for him to say – it was me the griffin was closing in on. I mean, of all the humans, in all of Romana, why was it so set on eating me?! It's not as though I had much meat on me. I leant forward, squeezing Titus's sides with my heels. It was now or never!

'Go Titus, go!'

The stallion rounded his shoulders, shifting his balance to his hind legs. Back straight, hips forward, I shortened the reins and prepared to jump.

I was Silvia Fortuna Juno De Luca, daughter of a war goddess and sister to a cyclops. Anything was possible . . .

CHAPTER 25

THE VERY ANNOYING GRIFFIN

ood news! I didn't snuff it! We made the jump! But with the griffin hot on our heels, I wasn't cancelling my coffin just yet.

'Faster, Titus,' I called. 'Faster!' If we could just make it into the forest, maybe we could lose old onion breath.

The griffin wasn't going to make it easy, though. Picking up speed, it swooped down and grabbed at my head, pulling out a massive clump of hair. *Like, no need!* I reached for my sword, waving it above me with one hand while gripping the reins with the other. It was time to give that griffin something to screech about!

'Come on, Titus! Come on!'

The griffin was right on top of us now. I stabbed at its hideous feet, gripping Titus with aching thighs. Seriously, my bum was killing me. And my arm was starting to hurt too. The jewelled gold sword might well be lighter than standard issue, but it was much heavier than the one I used for LARPing. On the plus side, it was sharper too. Sharp enough to make the griffin back off . . .

. . . but not for long.

It swooped down again, drool dripping from its rancid mouth.

Erg! All that dive-bombing was getting majorly annoying. Sitting up straight in the saddle, I swiped at the bird's incoming claws, its giant wings enveloping me in a tunnel of feathery putridness.

'Just leave it, will yer!' I swiped again.

The griffin screamed. Like, seriously screamed, as something sausage-shaped bounced off my head.

A talon.

I'd chopped off one of its talons. Which meant the warm stuff dripping down my cheek was blood! Eww!

The griffin was equally unhappy about the blood situation. It let out an ear-piercing shriek and dive-bombed me again, nearly knocking me from the saddle. It screeched, breath so rancid it stung my eyes, my world a watery blur of black, grey and silver. Which, trust me, isn't good when you're hurtling through no man's land with a frenzied griffin on your case.

This was it.

Goodbye cruel world.

It's been a blast—

But then the air grew damp, the stench of sulphuric onion replaced by fragrant pine. Titus slowed, whinnying proudly.

He'd done it – we'd reached the shelter of the forest.

Which was unfortunate for the griffin, who it appears did not have a functioning stop button and was going to have a major headache in the morning. The tree he'd rammed into wasn't faring any better. Hovering for a moment, it toppled to the ground, its thick leafy branches forming a cage around the writhing bird.

Breathing sharp and fast, I slid my sword back into its scabbard and wiped the blood from my face. I softened the reins and gave Titus a squeeze with my heels. See ya, Mr Onion-Breath! Moving on to problem number two.

That's if Titus didn't kill me first. It would seem he wasn't happy with just being horse jumper of the century, he also wanted to prove how awesome he was at slalom. Steam rising from his nostrils, he swerved in and out of the trees, bouncing me around like an ice cube in a blender.

'Slow down, Titus,' I pleaded. 'The griffin's gone!' But no matter how much I heaved on his reins or begged him to listen, he galloped on.

It was only when we reached the end of the forest and saw what was waiting for us beyond the trees that he finally stopped.

CHAPTER 26

BEYOND THE FOREST

I was getting used to weird stuff. I mean, my long-lost mother was a goddess, my dad had turned molten and for the past twenty-four hours I'd had to wipe my bum with a sponge on a stick. But none – and I repeat, NONE – of this had prepared me for the sight I was greeted with now.

At least ten-people deep, the wall of lava soldiers

stretched for as far as I could see in either direction, the hazy amber blur around their fearsome silhouettes splitting the scorched landscape in two. Suddenly, overcoming problem number two didn't seem quite so easy. Even Titus seemed unsure. Hovering in the treeline, he whinnied restlessly, eyes fixed on the wall of lava.

'What are we going to do now?' I said, stroking his damp neck.

Titus pawed the ground. Eyes wide, he reared up on to his hind legs, almost throwing me from the saddle, before darting out from behind the trees.

'Whoa!' I pulled on the reins, desperately trying to steer him back into the safety of the treeline. 'Titus, no!'

But he continued to bolt towards the soldiers.

'No, Titus, no!'

I heaved on his reins, trying to convince him to turn back into the trees. But it was like he'd sat on nettles or something. Hooves churning clouds of dirt behind him, he continued to charge forward.

'Stop, Titus!'

Zero response from Titus, but the lava soldiers were happy to give me their full attention. Glowing like hot coals, they lifted their spears, a zillion molten eyes boring into me. Well, maybe not quite a zillion, but like I had time to count them. I was too busy staring at the dragons! The glistening metal dragons perched on the giant stone pedestals positioned either side of the entrance to Vulcan's camp. Eyes flashing amber, they roared and stretched out their long silver necks, their mahoosive chain mail wings surprisingly delicate as they soared into the air.

'Turn round, Titus, please!'

A tiny bit of wee escaped as the dragons zoomed towards us. Gross, I know, but don't judge me. At least not until you've found yourself on an out-of-control horse pegging it towards a metal dragon the size of a double-decker bus.

'Please, Titus! Turn around!'

With the dragons right above us, Titus finally slowed. He reared, dancing on his back legs like a circus poodle before proceeding to run around in circles. *Thanks, Titus. Why don't you just sprinkle salt and pepper all over me too?* I was dragon fodder for sure.

I sighed, regret sitting heavy on my chest as I thought of all the things I'd never have the chance to do. Like putting smarties on my pizza or riding a motorbike while wearing a guinea pig onesie and a tiara. Oh well, at least I was right about the prophecy being a load of rubbish . . .

Except . . .

. . . the dragons flew right past me, performing a mega loop-de-loop before coming to a stop just above us, where they hovered, their whirring mechanical wings stirring the warm air like a giant fan.

Thunder roared and the sky flashed amber.

The soldiers lowered their spears, parting like the Red Sea to reveal a rugged lava field and the long straight road to Vulcan HQ.

Flames licking the sky, the dragons soared upwards again before darting into the depths of the camp.

Titus followed.

You what? I stared at the lava soldiers' expressionless faces – each and every one of them the same, as they saluted us through. They were all the same size too – their rigid metal bodies positioned in an identical pose. I had no idea where Dad was, but he wasn't one of these fellas.

With the dragons' wings beating out a low rhythmic drone, we continued towards the encroaching darkness. The fierce glow from the soldiers had dulled to a soupy yellow haze and the air was thick and humid. Titus had slowed to a canter, his coat damp with sweat, but he wasn't any less keen to move forward. And something was drawing me forward too.

For a start, I wanted to know what in the name of Jupiter was going on. Because it wasn't just the soldiers that didn't seem right. It was as though I'd entered some form of twilight world. There were no guards. No sleeping quarters. No weapon stores. Just a scarce lava bed, potted with craters and fissures – some of which released sulphuric steam that smelt almost as rotten as the griffin's breath. Athene Noctua was right – there was another truth. I had to at least try and uncover it.

Titus's hooves thudding against the rock, we continued across the endless field of lava. Maybe I should have been more frightened, especially when Titus followed the dragons down a steep uneven track that plummeted towards the sea, but the feeling of déjà vu I had was somehow reassuring. A cool salty breeze tugged at my hair. I leant into Titus, trusting the horse, trusting my gut just like Mrs Burden had told me too. If Vulcan wanted me dead, he'd had enough opportunities, right? Instead, here I was being escorted by his very own dragons.

The churning sea flickering amber and yellow, I gripped the reins as shingle crunched under Titus's hooves. The cove was exactly as Romulus had said it would be. Black basalt cliffs lined a windswept beach, the bay the shape of a squashed croissant. Slap bang in the centre of the cove, two burning cauldrons marked the start of the causeway, a row of flickering oil lamps dotted along the weathered rock until they reached the gaping black mouth of the cave. The island that housed the cave was bigger than I expected, a mini pumice-stone mountain jutting angrily from the waves, its peak swallowed by mist.

Titus continued forward. Letting out a high-pitched screech, the dragons hovered for a second before zooming upwards into the night sky and landing on the daunting cliffs at the far end of the beach. Thunder clapped and Titus pulled on his bit as we were enveloped in inky darkness. Lightning split the sky in two, and the oil lamps burst back into life. I braced myself.

There, standing on the shore, was Vulcan.

CHAPTER 27

MEETING UNCLE VULCAN

Well, at least I think it was Vulcan. He looked just like the images I'd seen . . . except he was smiling. Really smiling, like he'd just won his body weight in flamingo tongues or something. Which, trust me, would have been a lot of flamingo tongues. He was at least seven foot tall, and his muscles made Hercules look like Mr Bean. His brilliant-white tunic glimmering in the moonlight, he stepped closer, dark curly hair springing in tight spirals from beneath a conical skullcap, and an oversized gold bumbag slung over his shoulder. *Mmm*, I guess his beard was a bit long, but he was hardly Dumbledore, and it was much less unruly than Bellona had made out.

'Silvia,' he said, holding out his spade-like hand. 'Groovy to finally meet you.'

He really did seem pleased. Like, mega pleased. But I wasn't ready to shake his hand just yet.

Vulcan shrugged. 'Fair enough, cupcake,' he said. 'You still see through Bellona's eyes. But lean further into your intuition and you'll understand all is not as it seems.' Looking up at the moon, he clapped his hands together, opening them again to reveal a large juicy fig. 'Titus, my old friend!' he said, feeding him the fig. 'It's good to see you!'

Old friend? My neck hairs prickled.

'Now, let's get you comfortable.' Vulcan clapped again, and the intricately crafted firepits scattered around the beach burst into life. Turning towards the sea, he put his not-so-little finger and thumb to his mouth and whistled.

A nymph-like creature sprung from the waves. Her pearlescent catsuit as dry as dragon breath, she flicked her bottle-green hair over her shoulder and bowed.

'Good evening, Neso. Sorry to bother you, but do you mind seeing to our pal Titus here? He needs a good rub down and a nice cool drink. Ooh, and maybe you could find him a little blankie.' Vulcan tickled Titus under the chin. 'Yes, he says a little blankie would be groovy.'

A little blankie? I'd give him a little blankie, all right. Him and Vulcan had set me up!

But I guess, deep down, I knew that already. I knew it before I'd even left Camp Bellona. Titus chose me. While I was undecided, he had a plan. And something was telling me I had to go with it – that I needed to hear what Vulcan had to say.

'Come, Silvia,' he said. 'Titus needs to chillax. And you must be ready for a sit-down too.'

I slid down from the horse, black shingle

spraying as my sandals sank into the stones; stones worn over many years, each with their own story. What was Vulcan's?

Running her tongue over her fanged teeth, Neso waited for me to steady myself before reaching for Titus's reins. Eyes black and round, she put the hermit crab shell she wore on a long chain around her neck to her lips and blew, the lyrical sound mimicking the gentle roll of the surf. The sea grew still, and a second nymph rose from the waves, carrying a blanket and a bucket.

'Evening, Maira,' smiled Vulcan. 'Titus says thank you for looking after him.'

A sudden gust of wind tore at my tunic. Vulcan's expression changed, his brow furrowing. I followed his gaze.

Like, how many nymphs? Green hair decorated with starfish and seashells, they floated in the shallows, pale skin translucent in the moonlight.

'And remember, ladies,' Vulcan asserted. 'Silvia is our guest. There will be no sport tonight. No matter how this goes.'

The moon-kissed nymphs hissed and retreated into the waves. Neso and Maira nodded and led Titus towards a giant firepit. Humming in time with the sea, they began to rub him down with straw. The glow from the crackling firepit made their catsuits shimmer.

'This way, Silvia,' said Vulcan, rubbing his hands together excitedly. 'We have so much to catch up on.'

Biting my lip, I glanced towards the causeway and the sea cave where the sacred arrow waited – in the opposite direction to which Vulcan was leading me.

'The arrow is all yours, buttercup, but you won't find it in there. Not since old Dragonso developed arthritis and his fire valves began to stiffen.' He glanced over towards Neso and Maira. 'That was why I had to reposition it. I mean, would you trust those guys with the future of civilization?'

Probably not. But the big question was, could I trust Vulcan? I mean, did he really expect me to believe he was going to just hand me the arrow?

There was only one way to find out, I suppose. I followed him down the beach and away from the causeway, our path lit by parallel rows of bronze torches that ignited automatically as we approached. The salty air was tinged with the taste of smoke and sulphur.

Struggling to keep up in the shifting shingle, I wondered if the myths were true. If Vulcan's limp really was the result of his very own mum – *my supposed grandmother!* – throwing him off Mount Etna. And was his inner fire really as fierce as the myths said? His anger sparking flames of destruction or even spilling as lava when he got really annoyed? Maybe I should have thought this through!

'Are you OK, cupcake?' Vulcan said as we approached another gaping cave at the far end of the beach. 'Only, you haven't said much.'

I shrugged. 'I came here to listen.' In truth, I was too busy trying to stop my brain from exploding to string a sentence together.

'Fair enough. I guess your mind must be all over

177

the taberna! I mean, cosmic, man – one minute you're being told to eat your vegetables back in Once Brewed, the next you're immortal!'

'I'm not immortal.' And Dad never told me to eat my vegetables. It was usually the other way around.

Vulcan smiled. 'Well, maybe not yet. But in the end, nobody can resist the draw of the nectar.'

Not yet? Seriously, my head was so full of questions my neck was going to snap.

But my questions were going to have to wait – Vulcan had already reached the cave. And my overloaded brain, well that had moved on to the next big question: like, how could this possibly be Vulcan's command centre? Bunting danced in the breeze and half-hearted fairy lights clung to a pair of scraggy potted fig trees, positioned either side of a weathered sun lounger. Next to the lounger there was a sun-bleached Coca-Cola parasol that looked like it had been stolen from a beer garden, underneath which sat a rusty barbecue and a faded ice bucket full of empty pop bottles. Yes, pop bottles.

In Romana. See what I mean about all the questions?

The inside of the cave was just as unexpected. What with the red and blue plastic lemonade crates lining the porch area, and the rough weave rug littered with sweet wrappers and bottle tops.

Vulcan shrugged, the flickering oil lamp behind him casting dark shadows around the porch. 'Some things are just too good to leave in Britannia, don't you think? I've got some turkey twizzlers too, if you fancy one?' He clapped his hands and the circular stone forge burst into life, lighting up the inner cave. 'They'll only take a minute on the grill.'

Erg, like, no thanks. I'd rather take my chances with Bellona's stuffed dormice. This place made an orc-sty look hygienic. It wasn't just the porch that was a tip – there was stuff everywhere. As well as all his blacksmith tools, there was a penny farthing, a drum kit, piles of dog-eared paperbacks and at least five different gaming consoles. The poster of the Dalai Lama next to the primrose surfboard was particularly random. Coupled with all the firepits and oil lamps, the cave was an accident waiting to happen.

'Sorry about the mess,' Vulcan said, puffing up the cushion on the indigo couch that faced out to the sea. 'It's amazing how much stuff you collect over the centuries.' Squeezing past the oil drum firepit, he removed the lid from a faded gold cool box and pulled out a selection of drinks, ice spilling on to the stone floor and bouncing under the coffin-shaped metal box leaning against the wall of crates.

'What is that?' I asked.

'It's a mould. Every single one of my peacekeepers is cast from it. I figured if all are created equal, nobody has the right to control. Groovy, hey!'

'You mean your lava army?'

'An army is trained to fight, but my guys were created to deter war – to protect the arrow from those who might seek to do harm. They cannot strike first.' He sighed, the glow from the furnace creating an amber haze around him. 'But enough talk of this – refreshment before business. Now, where's my bottle opener?' He searched the hostess trolley half-heartedly, before clearing the magazines and record sleeves off the coffee table.

That's when I saw them.

The pile of papyrus posters with my face all over them.

'Please, Silvia, sit. Now, what do you fancy? Vimto, maybe?'

Was he for real? I folded my arms and gave him my best dirty look. But Vulcan just shrugged his shoulders. Delving into the icebox again, he pulled out another pop bottle and wiped it on his pristine white-and-gold tunic.

'Fanta, maybe, then?' He cracked off the lid with his teeth.

'No thank you!' So much for Athene Noctua and her other truths. I'd really hoped she was right. That there was another explanation. But the posters on the table spoke for themselves.

Vulcan's face went all scrunchy, his nose twitching. 'But you must!' he said. 'I can see the thirst on your lips. Hospitium demands I offer you refreshment.'

The hospitium thing again. Kidnap half of Romana. Rage war on your sister. Or put a price on a child's head. But whatever you do, don't forget to offer your visitors a snack!

'Look, Vulcan—'

'Uncle Vulcan, please!' He placed the Fanta on the bronze tripod table next to me. 'Come on, now, spit it out. What's pulling on your goatee?'

'Oh my gods!' Blood thundered in my ears. Bellona was right. He really was infuriating. 'Just tell me what you've done with my dad!'

'You think I've kidnapped your father?'

'I know you did.' I pointed at the posters. 'And you put a price on my head.'

'Those are some far-out accusations from a mortal. I thought you'd come here to listen.'

'I've heard enough. I want the arrow. Now!'

Steam rose from the neck of the Coke bottle Vulcan was nursing, the glass turning molten and dripping on to his gold gladiator sandal.

I backed towards the door. What was I doing shouting at the god of fire like that?!

'Chill, man.' Vulcan wiped the molten glass from his foot with a giant purple and gold handkerchief. 'I'm a pacifist. I'm not going to hurt you.'

'A pacifist?'

'Yes, I had a revolution of conscience back in the third century. Love and respect all the way. That's what Romana was meant to be all about; a brave New World where we could start again. All that empire-building, the slavery, the pilfering, the crucifixions – it just wasn't groovy. I wanted something better for the mortals – Rome but without the bad bits, a parallel realm to start afresh. Bellona promised she wanted it too. I should have known it was only a matter of time until she'd crave war again.'

I had to admit he was convincing. His eyes had a wistful look, the amber glow replaced by a blackness that reflected the sea. But the posters on the table told a different story.

'You don't believe me, do you?'

I shrugged. 'Just tell me where my dad is.'

Vulcan picked up one of the papyrus posters and

held it out in front of me. 'To really see, you must open your mind as well as your eyes.'

'Far out, man! Now tell me where my dad is! I know you've taken him.'

'And I suppose you heard that from your mother?' Vulcan sighed and sat down on the couch, his eyes burning with fire. 'I was really hoping you'd have worked it out for yourself by now, buttercup. But perhaps I was wrong to trust this to the universe. Perhaps I need to spell it out for you?'

'Spell what out?'

He handed me the poster, pointing at the faint smudge on the bottom. 'That I might be the god of fire, but it's Bellona's pants that are on fire.'

CHAPTER 28

PANTS ON FIRE

Taking the poster from Vulcan, I breathed in another gulp of dense, smoky air. I felt like the cave was closing in on me. The flickering shadows laughed and sneered – *you total gnat brain*, they said!

And they were right! The mark was faint – barely visible until I held the papyrus up to the light – but the traces of the wax stamp were there all the same: *Temple of Bellona*. The posters had been issued and approved by Bellona's very own office.

'But she's my mum. Why would she put a price on my head?'

Vulcan sighed, his forehead crumpling like an elderly pug. 'I'm sorry, Silvia. I truly am—'

'Taking Dad too. It just doesn't make sense.'

'It makes perfect sense when you think about it. She knew you'd come after him. That you'd do anything to save your dad ... especially if she could convince you your big bad tyrant of an uncle had it in for the whole family.'

'But my own mother, lying to me like that.'

Vulcan shrugged. 'All's fair in love and war, as the power-hungry say.' Lacing his fingers together, he placed his hands behind his head and leant back on the sofa. 'Personally, I think relationships should be built on mutual trust and respect, but history has taught me I'm in the minority. Gods know I tried to make my fire a force for good. I persuaded Bellona to help me fight a new war; a war against poverty, suffering and injustice. It was beautiful, man, truly beautiful. Until she got bored.'

'So, you're telling me this whole mess is because Bellona got bored?' I took a gulp of Fanta. Suddenly, I needed ALL the sugar!

'Pretty much. Though don't be too hard on her, cupcake. War's in her DNA, just as fire is in mine. It pulses through her veins and drives her every desire. That's why we invented LARPing, so she could feed the need without hurting anybody.'

Whoa! Was he really claiming to have invented LARPing? He was taking things too far now!

'It kept her amused for a while,' he continued. 'But then she started to complain. Said it was nothing like the thrill of a real battle. The power and excitement that came with building an empire.'

It was then I knew for certain he was speaking the truth. 'The glorious thrill of war', Bellona had called it at the celebration party.

Vulcan reached for another bottle of pop. 'She wanted us to start a *proper* war together – claim back the ancient Roman Empire that was rightfully ours. And when I said no, she told me to go hug a tree. Said I was a big beardy spoilsport and I'd regret it when she put my fire out once and for all.'

My stomach sank even further. I'd heard Bellona say the exact same words.

'I thought she was just mouthing off at first,' Vulcan continued. 'We'd fallen out before, but she always came round after a century or two. But then I received word that the Prima Sibyl's founding prophecy was true. Bellona hadn't been going off to Britannia to LARP. That little sneak had been busy spawning her very own army of demigods – an army of demigods that would allow her to rebuild the empire and gain back the power she so craved.'

'Spawning?' I felt like I'd been whacked in the stomach with Vulcan's hammer.

'I'm sorry. It sounds awful when you put it like that.'

On uncertain legs, I stood up, pistachio shells sticking to the soles of my sandals. The shadows pointed and jeered. I had to get out of there. I had to find out what Bellona had done with Dad.

'Please, Silvia, wait! It doesn't matter where you're from, it's where you're going. You are the one who will make this right.'

'Stop it!' I yelled, heading towards the mouth of the cave. 'Stop it!' The prophecy was wrong. How could I possibly fix this when I was nothing more than a living, breathing avatar in Bellona's very own version of Rome Play?

A thunderous roar stopped me in my tracks as Vulcan's furnace flashed, filling the cave with a blinding light.

'Oh, just quit with the poor-little-me act,' said a familiar voice. 'Do you want to save Romana or not?'

CHAPTER 29

PREPARING TO STRIKE

Athene Noctua! Was I dreaming again? Had this whole thing been one huge nightmare? I pinched myself, hoping to wake up to the sound of Dad pottering about downstairs – doing his sword drills, maybe, or polishing his armour.

But no such luck.

I was still there inside Vulcan's cave and, worse

still, that know-it-all owl was there too. Well, her head was at least. Or rather a giant holographic flame-licked version of her head that was somehow inside the furnace.

'Athene Noctua!' said Vulcan, a smile warming his face. 'It's been a while.'

Flames flicked from the owl's beaky nostrils. 'Couple of millennia, by my reckoning. But whose fault is that?'

Vulcan's smile drooped. 'I'm sorry I didn't visit. But you know how it is when people break up.'

'Of course I know how it is. I know everything. But it still hurts, you just disappeared like that. Anyway, all that's history. I came to speak to the mortal. Word on the mountain is, Bellona is preparing to strike.'

'Preparing to strike?' I made my way towards the furnace.

'Yes,' said Athene Noctua. 'Attack. Charge. Go ballistic!'

'But she knows she won't get through my defences ... not unless—'

'Cool your **calcei**, big man. The kid's no conspirator. Bellona doesn't need to get through your defences. She's taking the battle to Britannia.'

Like, what! Did the owl really say Britannia?

'Yes, Britannia,' she repeated.

'But she hates Britain.' Vulcan scratched his beard. 'The climate gives her chilblains.'

'Oh, it's not too bad this time of year. And things will soon heat up once her army arrives at Housesteads.'

Housesteads? As in Housesteads Fort, and the Rome Play site?

'Yes, Silvia! Honestly, what's with all the repeats? Have you got flamingo tongues stuck in your ears or something?'

What was it with Romanans and all the flamingo tongues, more like it? I stepped closer to the furnace, the searing heat forcing me back again. 'But why would Bellona attack Housesteads?'

'She knows you're wise to her, chick. Figures you'll soon give her the arrow when you see what she's up to.'

'But the LARPers – Rome Play opens today. They'll think it's part of the game.'

'Exactly.' The furnace crackled. 'Especially given she's planning to use your dad to bait them. That's if Orcus can remember where he's put him. He's another one who should have retired years ago.'

Panic rose in my chest. 'Orcus? But the Underworld is for dead people!'

'Which it is why it is such a great hiding place for the living,' sighed Vulcan.

That sneaky, lying, war-thirsty poop head. I'd had enough of my so-called mother's games. 'How do I get to the Underworld—?'

'Erg, by dying,' said Athene Noctua. 'And I really can't have you snuffing it on my watch. Leave it to me. My wisdomnous will find Ben.'

I legged it back to the sofa and picked up my bow and arrow.

'Wait!' called Vulcan. 'You heard Athene.'

'The LARPers,' I said. 'I have to warn them!'

*

The sun was beginning to rise as I strode out of Vulcan's cave and on to the beach. A perfect semi-circle of fire, it cast a glow over the slumbering sea, the clouds streaked with orange and purple. It was as though the whole world was burning. I searched the volcanic bay for Titus, and spotted him across the beach.

'Wait,' Vulcan called again behind me. 'We need to talk tactics.'

'There's no time!' Picking up speed, I continued towards Titus. 'I have to warn them now!'

'Silvia!'

I scurried onwards, as fast as I could. Which wasn't overly fast given the shifting pebbles.

'Well, at least take the arrow!'

'What?' I turned around. 'You want me to give Bellona the arrow?'

'Of course not, but if you are going to insist on going on ahead, I'd at least like you to have a fighting chance.' Vulcan clapped his hands together twice and a low rumbling echo reverberated around the beach. 'Which is why I'd also like to introduce you to a friend of mine.'

No way! The glimmering black cliffs were literally tearing open. From the cavernous hole bolted a wolf . . . a huge, lollopy iron wolf with molten amber eyes and pointy ears that swivelled like NASA satellite dishes. It paused to howl at the paling moon then started to run around in circles, chasing its tail.

'Lupa!' cried Vulcan. 'Over here!'

The wolf bounded towards us, her beaten-bronze tongue flopping out the side of her mouth. Shingle spraying like confetti, she skidded to a stop just centimetres from my toes, bouncing up and down on the spot before lunging at Vulcan. Paws pressed against his shoulders, she licked his face as though it was her last dinner, before running around in circles again, howling.

'Calm, Lupa!' said Vulcan. 'I have an important job for you.'

The wolf wagged her tail and sat down, her excited panting sending steam clouds into the dawn sky.

'Good girl!' Vulcan patted the wolf on the copper-wire scruff around her neck. 'Silvia, meet Lupa, my latest prototype. Isn't she just the grooviest?'

Reaching up, I ran my fingers over the wolf's powerful shoulders, the studded iron panels warm and smooth between my fingers. She turned her head and licked my nose, her paper-thin tongue smoother than I expected. I guess she *was* pretty groovy.

'Lupa,' said Vulcan. 'This is my niece, Silvia. She needs a little favour.' He leant into the wolf, whispering something into her ear.

Lupa stood up and wagged her tail.

'Groovy.' Vulcan rubbed his hands together like he was warming up for something. 'She says she'd be honoured to take you.'

'Take me?'

Smiling like a teacher who'd just broken up for the summer holidays, Vulcan clicked his fingers. 'Now, you might just want to stand back there, cupcake. Lupa, activate flight mode.'

There was a whirring noise and Lupa shuddered. Body rigid, the panels on her back split open to reveal a studded metal saddle with a small round grab handle like you get on see-saws. Saddle clicking into position, the wolf's tail began to whirl. Faster and faster it went, whizzing around like a helicopter blade, Lupa panting excitedly as she hovered just above the ground.

'Come on, buttercup,' said Vulcan. 'I'll give you a leg-up.'

I didn't need asking twice. I mean, a flying wolf! *Get in!* Plus, as much as I hated to admit it, Vulcan was right – I needed his help. Warning the LARPers was not going to end this. Using his cupped hands as a mounting block, I threw my leg over Lupa, careful to avoid her whirring tail.

'Ready, Lupa?' Vulcan stuck his finger up Lupa's nostril and shut his eyes, veins glowing orange through his godly skin. Lupa was glowing too, her body growing warm. 'There you go – fully charged. You'll be at Housesteads before you know it. Warn the LARPers but then hide and wait for backup. I'll be right behind you as soon as I've charged the lava soldiers.'

Lupa threw her head back and howled, her whole body tilting as she jerked forward. I gripped the grab handle. Mmm, maybe this wasn't such a good idea after all!

'Stop!' Athene Noctua. The little owl was back to her normal feathery self, her speckled plumage rippling in the breeze. Looking down her beak at us, she flapped her wings, hovering above like she was treading water. 'Aren't you both forgetting something?'

'Oops.' Vulcan reached inside his oversized bumbag and pulled out the arrow, pausing for a second to polish the golden shaft on his tunic before handing it to me.

It was lighter than I expected. Smaller too, the arrowhead not much bigger than my thumbnail. I ran my finger over the extravagant crimson fletching.

'Phoenix feathers, cupcake. The god struck by this arrow will be reborn in mortal form.'

'Well, unless you hit them in the head,' said Athene Noctua. 'Then they'll snuff it, for sure.'

Vulcan shrugged. 'Which is why it's a good job Silvia is such an excellent shot.'

'What? You want me to shoot my own mother?' They had to be kidding, right?

'Only if absolutely necessary,' said Vulcan. 'I'm still hoping she'll back down. She knows the power of the arrow. That's why she wants it so much – so she can stop any god that would stand in her way.'

'And if she doesn't back down?'

Vulcan looked at Athene Noctua. Who looked at me. Who looked at Vulcan. 'Then the Undecided must make her decision.'

CHAPTER 30

DON'T LOOK DOWN

Wow! My Uncle Vulcan was not wrong – Lupa really was super-groovy fast, man! Tail whirling, legs doing that same lollopy-lopy thing they did when she was running, she cut effortlessly through the air. The sacred arrow stored safely in my quiver, I clung tight to her handle, and it wasn't long before the distant yellow of the cornfields was

replaced by trees, the trees replaced by red-roofed villas, and the villas by the sprawling mass of Romana City.

We were flying lower now, the early-morning mist dancing around me, as Lupa clumsily skirted the temples and basilica of the forum. How she missed the weathervane on the senate house, I don't know!

'Careful, Lupa,' I said, cringing as the clangs from my encouraging shoulder pats reverberated off the tiled rooftops. So much for sneaking up on the enemy. Not that the clanging bothered Lupa. Ears swivelling like radar detectors, she kept her eyes fixed on the horizon, clouds of steam rising from her mouth and mingling with the mist.

And then there it was before me, sitting uncomfortably on a scrap of land just beyond the row of taverns on the western edge of the city: the triumphal arch, the gateway that would lead me back to Housesteads – and whatever that would bring.

That's if Lupa didn't kill me first! Ears pinned,

she plummeted towards the arch like a god who'd been chucked off Mount Olympus. My stomach plummeted too, last night's dinner bouncing off my kneecaps, as she launched herself through the gateway, my head so close to the keystone I almost lost my scalp.

'Careful, Lupa! Please!'

Lupa turned her head towards me, her tongue flailing as she tried to lick me.

'Concentrate, Lupa!'

The metal wolf howled and rose upwards again, soaring above the valley. That's when I saw it – the sea of cloaks turning the windswept slopes of Whin Sill crimson. Bellona's armies had almost reached the Rome Play camp! Lupa whimpered. In the distance I caught a glimpse of the special stadium that had been built for the Harry Styles gig, a line of eager fans already looping around the metal barriers. They had no idea what was coming their way if I didn't stop Bellona. And neither did the LARPers.

'Hurry, Lupa!'

The dank mist swirling around us, Lupa closed in on the camp and my heart sank at the sight of the soggy tents and roughly painted building facades. The dream Dad had worked so hard to bring to life was now a living nightmare. It got worse. Huddled together in the fort were the LARPers. The drizzle soaking their tunics, they gripped their fake swords and spears, eyes fixed on the tsunami of scarlet flooding the hillside below.

'Kenzo!' He was right at the front of the swarming mass, next to Chitra. Closer now, I could see there were around fifty of them – mostly crew and Dad's local LARP group. 'You need to get everyone out of here!'

Nothing. I clung tight to the handle as Lupa landed on the grass in front of the south gate. She shuddered and shut down.

'Kenzo! Chitra! Please, you have to listen to me! Get out of here now!'

If Dad's closest friends were shocked by the site of me plonking down in front of them on a flying metal wolf they didn't show it. There wasn't much of a reaction from the other LARPers either, who continued to focus on the encroaching legionaries.

I slid down from Lupa, sandals squelching in the sodden grass. 'Are you listening? You all need to get out of here right now.'

My protests swallowed by the noise, I legged it towards Kenzo, holding my hand in the air to signal I was out of character. 'Kenzo, listen to me, please! You have to get everyone out of here. This isn't what it seems.'

'Nothing ever is, Livi.' He looked down over the low crumbling walls and winked. 'That's what makes life so interesting.'

Profound. But if I'd wanted flaky wisdomnous, I'd have stayed in Vulcan's cave. I climbed up on to the wall and into the fort. 'Chitra! Somebody listen to me, please!'

'It's OK, Livi,' said Chitra, her eyes reflecting the sea of crimson that was creeping ever closer. 'We've got this.'

Kenzo lifted his sword. 'We *so* do!'

They so didn't. Bellona's armies were almost upon

us. The dull wallop of the centurion's pace-sticks growing ever nearer as they marched up the slope.

'Kenzo!' I put my hands on his shoulders and pushed, trying to edge him backwards. 'You need to leave now. People are going to die.'

'Whoa!' Kenzo steadied himself. 'Chill, Livi. I've not seen you this hyped since I bought you that massive blue raspberry slushy and you cried because your poop turned green!'

Seriously, was he ever going to let me live that down?! I flung my arms in the air in frustration. 'Why won't anybody listen to me?'

'Cool it!' The smell of a fresh spring morning filled my nostrils. The scent was followed by a sharp yap as Mrs Burden eased her way in between Kenzo and Chitra, Kevin following at her heel. 'How exactly do yer think that's helping? Leave the fire to yer uncle!'

'But we need to get everyone away from here.' What did she think she was playing at? She might as well sacrifice the LARPers at Bellona's altar herself.

Mrs Burden tightened the fastener on her plastic rain hood, her petrol-blue mac buttoned tightly over her stola. 'They know the score. They're mortals, not babies.'

'Yeah,' said Kenzo, fist-bumping Mrs Burden. 'Tina here's filled us in. We've got your back, Livi! Always!'

The LARPers cheered. Some of them linked arms and began to dance around in circles.

'Stop it!' I cried. 'This isn't a game!'

'Everything's a game,' said Kenzo. 'Some games are just more dangerous than others. We can't let the bad guys win.'

'But this isn't your fight. My Uncle Vulcan will be here any moment—'

'Open yer eyes, child,' spat Mrs Burden. 'He's too late.'

CHAPTER 31

ANNIHILATION!

I swallowed, fighting back the urge to puke. Bellona's armies were less than the length of a football pitch away. And there were like literally zillions of them – red-caped legionaries in the middle, cavalry on their wings, and the auxiliaries, with their oval shields and green tunics, at the rear.

Kevin jumped on to the wall, his hackles rising.

He looked back at me, head cocked, brown eyes quizzical.

'Now might be a good time to fulfil your destiny, lass,' said Mrs Burden.

A horn blew and the valley fell silent. Bowing their heads, Bellona's personal guards parted to reveal her chariot.

'Silvia Fortuna Juno De Luca!' she bellowed, bringing her horses to a stop halfway between her troops and the fort. 'You have been a very naughty girl. How exactly is this coming straight back?'

Naughty?! Bit rich coming from her . . . and how did she know I wasn't coming back? She hadn't exactly given me much time.

Bellona's turquoise cape billowed in the wind, her four white stallions whinnying nervously in the unfamiliar drizzle. 'I mean it, Silvia! This is your last chance. Hand over the sacred arrow and take your rightful place beside me or I'll send you to the naughty cloud once and for all.'

Kevin howled. The LARPers raised their weapons.

'As for your silly little mortal chums, tell them to stand down or I'll annihilate every single one of them!'

Annihilation . . . that didn't sound good! Where were Vulcan and the lava soldiers?

Not that Bellona's threats bothered the LARPers.

'Supprime tuum stultiloquium!' yelled Kenzo. *Stop your blathering!* Nice! And he wasn't finishing there. He beat his chest and let out a guttural war cry, Kevin and the LARPers joining in before forming a wall around me. Some of the regulars from Dad's LARP group jumped on to the wall of the fort, standing as proud and defiant as the ancient Caledonian warriors it had been built to retain. They'd held strong despite the odds too.

And that's what I had to do.

Hold strong.

And believe.

'Thanks, everyone. But I have to face her.' I had to try and make this right. Shivering, I pushed my way through the LARPers and climbed on to the wall.

Bellona smiled. She edged her chariot forward. '**Bona puella**, now, down you come.'

'Unlikely!' I stood up tall. The drizzle had turned to fat raindrops. They beat against my face and ran down my neck in icy trickles. 'Tell your troops to stand down. It's not too late to find a peaceful solution.'

Bellona's laughter echoed around the silent valley. 'What? And spoil everyone's fun?! You were born for this, Silvia. Together we will rebuild the empire and bask in her glory.'

'The empire's over. But there are other ways to find glory—'

'Piff, you've been spending too much time with your uncle. Now, give me the arrow!'

'You know I can't do that.'

Bellona sighed. She signalled to Potty-Mouth and the Praetorian Guards separated. I held my breath, trying to control my reactions. There they were, armed and ready, Bellona's very own army of demigods – my own brothers and sisters pitched against me. I felt like part of me had died.

'Cease this at once, Silvia,' said Bellona. 'Your place is with your family. Bring forth the arrow and stand beside us! Together, we shall be invincible!'

I stared at my brothers and sisters. Romulus and Remus were at least five shades paler than when I'd left them. Tiber looked like he'd eaten something dodgy too. He was trotting on the spot next to the twins, Poly and Felix holding hands in front of him. They didn't want this either! I had to stay strong for all of us.

'Never!' I cried. 'Stand down, Bellona. You know you can't win. The prophecy says it is me who will decide this.'

'Very well.' Bellona's aura sizzled red. 'Annihilation it is. Romulus, bring forward the sagittarii!'

CHAPTER 32

TAKING BRITANNIA!

'No, Mamma, please!' Felix charged towards Bellona's chariot. He was carrying Scylla, the water in her new bronze-gilded jar sloshing. 'Livi, please! Do what Mamma says.'

Bellona held her arm out to the side, signalling for Romulus to pause. 'Listen to your brother, Silvia. It really is the only way.'

Blood pounding in my ears, I searched the valley for signs of Vulcan.

'Something's wrong, lass,' said Mrs Burden, climbing on to the wall beside me. 'I can feel it in me waters. It's down to you to fix this.'

'Coventina!' Bellona shook her head. 'You stand with the Undecided? Is this because I sent you to the sticks? How about I give you Sicilia or something? Somewhere nice and sunny for Bert to live out his final days.'

Kevin snarled. Hackles raised, he leant forward and bared his teeth.

'No thank you,' said Mrs Burden, patting the little woolly dog. 'I like it just fine 'ere in Once Brewed, with me bingo and me reading group. Listen to the girl, Bellona. The empire's over.'

'So be it. Romulus, proceed!'

'But perhaps Coventina is right, mother,' Romulus said, addressing the troops as much as the war goddess. 'Sister has offered an olive branch—'

Bellona's aura flickered, forming clouds of steam around her. 'I didn't come here to negotiate. I came to take Britannia!'

'Of course, Mother,' said Remus. 'But perhaps bloodshed is not the best way to win the loyalty of the mortals. Things have moved on since the empire.'

'Why, you miserable serpent-haired loincloths!' Rummaging in her cloak, Bellona pulled out a cotton reel. She blew on it and it unravelled, a sliver of gleaming silver thread looping itself around Romulus's and Remus's ankles before attaching itself to her chariot.

'But Mamma-Dude!' protested Tiber.

'Quiet, you overgrown pony! Let this be a warning to anyone who would defy me!'

The chain around Romulus's and Remus's ankles turned molten, and their snakes screeched in pain. A ripple of liquid silver spreading upwards from their feet, the twins stood still as statues, their mouths frozen in a scream.

Poly made to charge at Bellona, but Tiber grabbed her tunic and held her close, Felix holding on tight to Scylla's jar, cheeks smudged with tears.

'Well done, Tiber,' said Bellona. 'It would be a shame for the little ones to get hurt now, wouldn't it.' She blew her horn. 'Sagittarii, what are you waiting for? Take the girl out. Now!'

Hands shaking like a flamingo inside a Roman delicatessen, I reached for the sacred arrow. 'Please, don't make me do this. Call your soldiers off. This is your opportunity to be truly great—'

A ripple of unease spread through Bellona's legions as a pink sparkly helicopter circled above. *Harry Styles arriving for soundcheck, maybe?* Whoever it was, they were having a proper good nosy at the Rome Play site.

And Bellona's troops did not like it one bit. Panicked sagittarii pointed their arrows towards the sky and edged backwards, the mumbling legions behind them raising their swords as they talked in frenzied whispers about the metal bird.

'Hold your positions,' cried Bellona. 'You superstitious pumpkins!'

Oh my Greco-Roman gods, that was it! Maybe I didn't have to shoot my own mother after all.

While Bellona's bewildered troops were still pre-occupied with the helicopter, I drew Kenzo, Mrs Burden and Chitra into a huddle. In hurried whispers, I told them my plan. The plan that was so ridiculous it might just work.

If anyone could make it happen, Kenzo could. Meanwhile, it was over to Mrs Burden to buy us some time . . .

CHAPTER 33

PUDDING CLUB

The helicopter circled again, disappearing into the distance, and Bellona's troops finally grew calm. Well, when I say calm, there were still a lot of white faces and shaky knees, but at least nobody on the front line was crying any more. So much for all those Latin sayings about bravery! No wonder Bellona was fuming.

'Sagittarii,' she cried. 'For the final time! Load your weapons and take aim! **Mortems** omnibus!' *Death to all!*

'Please, Mamma!' cried Felix. 'You promised you wouldn't hurt them!'

'Don't worry, lad.' Mrs Burden winked. 'I've got this!' The trails of her fancy stola flapping in the wind, she raised her arms out in front of her and began to make circles with her hands. Foamy liquid spun around them like whirlpools.

'Sagittarii,' raged Bellona. 'Fire!'

Eyes closed, Mrs Burden bent her elbows and thrust her arms forward, her jowls vibrating as a wall of water formed in front of us just in time to deflect the shower of arrows.

'Again!' Bellona yelled. 'Altius Dirigite!' *Aim higher!*

The archers loaded their bows.

'Fire!'

Mrs Burden clicked her tongue, her skin glistening as she drew moisture from the atmosphere. The wall of water grew higher, convexing and stretching to form an impenetrable dome over the fort and the LARPers. Honestly, it was brilliant. Like being inside a mahoosive snow globe. Only instead of snow, there were giant weightless raindrops floating around us like space junk. It would have been great fun – especially with Kevin running around snapping and snarling at the raindrops – if it weren't the only thing keeping us alive.

The dome rippled as the sound of an air horn blasted across the valley.

'What the monkeys?' said Chitra.

What the monkeys indeed! It wasn't just any old horn. It was one of those really annoying musical jobbies. And it was playing 'Baby Shark'!

It sounded again, Bellona's troops separating to make way for . . .

. . . an . . .

. . . er . . .

. . . wait for it . . .

. . . mobility scooter.

A Harley Davidson mobility scooter, to be precise, that was storming up the hillside like a

Ferrari on Grand Prix day.

'Bert,' gasped Mrs Burden, the shield rippling again.

'Tina, what you playing at?' Mr Burden whacked the remaining archers out of the way with his gold walking stick. 'You promised to help me make a jam roly-poly!' With the pirate flag on the back of his scooter flying proudly, he pulled up next to Bellona's chariot. 'All right, Bea,' he said, raindrops rolling down the sleeve of his biker jacket as he lifted his flight goggles and rested them over his paisley bandana. 'Sorry to interrupt, like, but it's pudding club this afternoon. No pudding, no entry.'

Bellona rolled her eyes and thrashed her whip! 'Seize him, you donkeys. Have him delivered straight to the Underworld and tortured for all eternity.'

Mr Burden turned as grey as his long shaggy beard. 'Yer what? I was just about to invite you to pudding club too.'

'I'm afraid, Bert, your pudding days are over!'

Bellona cracked her whip again, the thong wrapping around Bert's arm and pulling him from his scooter. He landed awkwardly near her chariot, Potty-Mouth springing forward and pressing the tip of his sword against the old man's chest. Hackles raised, teeth bared, Kevin dived at the wall of water. He yelped as the impenetrable dome sent him bouncing backwards.

'Tiber!' Bellona snapped her fingers. 'Deliver him to Orcus immediately . . . unless, Coventina, you are ready to see sense? Your husband for the girl!'

The dome rippled again, the LARPers glancing nervously at each other as the roof dented. Kevin began to howl.

'Save the Undecided, Tina,' cried Mr Burden. 'We knew this day would come. Just find a way to get me one more slice of Battenberg cake and I'll happily take my leave of this place.'

'Quiet, you buffoon! What bit of eternal torture don't you get?' Bellona climbed down from her chariot and lifted her whip. The air sizzled with electricity as she brought it down on Bert, who let out a startled whimper.

The dome shook.

Water crashed down on us as fiercely as the waves crashing down on Ulysses and his crew after they scoffed the cattle of the sun. Only these waves just kept on coming. Knee-deep in murky liquid, I fought to catch my breath as the torrent of water rushed over the wall, forming a deep, muddy puddle in the hollow in front of the fort. *Kevin! Where's Kevin?* I thumped the air in relief as he surfaced, spluttering and coughing up water.

'Back away from the biker!' cried Mrs Burden. She was hovering in the air above the puddle, her mac and stola all floaty and billowy like a spectre.

'Enough!' Bellona's aura raged red. 'How dare you defy me, Coventina.' She pointed at Bert. 'Finish him—'

'Don't even think about it, wee-breath!' Potty-Mouth flew backwards into the front line as Mrs Burden shot a jet of water at his stomach. The goddess closed her eyes and fat raindrops rose upwards from the ground, forming thousands of cricket-ball sized globes that hovered in the air. Raising her arms, Mrs Burden thrust her hands forward, pummelling Bellona's front line with the water globes. Exhausted, she fell to the ground in a crumpled heap.

Aura crackling red, purple and turquoise, Bellona pointed her spear. Yikes, the Burdens were in for it now . . .

Except Bellona wasn't heading for Mrs Burden.

She was coming for me!

Spear aimed right at my head, she raged forward, staring at me in a way that made my stomach turn inside out. I reached into my quiver for the arrow.

'Enough! Cavalry, charge!'

'No!' Felix. He was still carrying Scylla, the water in her jar sloshing as he fumbled to undo the lid. 'I won't let you hurt Silvia!' he cried. Bellona's whip thrashing at his ankles, he threw himself at the puddle and eased the frenzied sea monster out of the jar.

Tentacles thrashed and teeth gnashed as Scylla plopped down into the water and began to grow.

And grow.

And grow.

'Felix, come on!' I reached for my brother's hand, water spraying as Scylla reared up to her full giganotosaurus size.

'Felix!'

Scylla let out a mighty roar. Which was kind of wasted, really, because the cavalry men were already halfway down the hill, their horses bucking and screaming as they retreated towards the portal.

'Here, Livi!' cried Kenzo, holding out his hand from on top of the wall.

'Felix, please! Come on!' I wasn't going anywhere without my brother.

'It's OK, Silvia.' Felix gave me a mischievous smile and tapped Scylla on one of her long necks. She made a weird purring noise, proffering a meaty blue tentacle. Steadying himself, Felix stepped on to the tentacle and the sea monster lifted him into the air.

'Felix! No!'

Making the OK sign, Felix stuck his arms up, back straight and elongated, like he was about to do a handstand. 'Fire!' he called.

Scylla roared. She flicked her giant tentacle and shot Felix into the clouds.

CHAPTER 34

SURPRISE!

A flash of blinding light turned the sky gold, blobs of green, purple and yellow floating in front of my eyelids. I rubbed my eyes and when I opened them again Felix had gone. And in his place there was a bird. A giant speckled bird with a long tail which looked like it had been dipped in chocolate. Wings pinned to its sides, the bird hovered for a moment before shooting towards the ground and doing a loop-de-loop above me.

Like, what? The bird had a human head! A human head that looked exactly like Felix!

'Surprise, Silvia,' called a familiar voice. 'My special talent!'

Eyes burning red, the Felix-bird-thing let out a high-pitched screech and fired a flurry of laser beams along the front line, forcing the soldiers backwards.

Bellona cracked her whip above her head. 'Felix Jupiter Volareisis, stop that this minute!'

Mud splattered around Bellona's ankles as Felix pummelled the ground with laser fire.

'Well, it looks like you've got it all in hand here,' said Mrs Burden, now back on her feet. She lifted Bert on to the back of the mobility scooter and plonked a soggy Kevin into the shopping basket, before easing herself into the seat. 'I need to get Bert and Kevin to the hospital. You'll be reet, lass, the Fates are on your side.' Shaking Bert's walking stick, Mrs Burden blasted the 'Baby Shark' air horn. 'Now out of me way, you lot!'

Felix fired another laser beam and the legionaries parted, clearing a path down the hill for Mrs Burden.

'Hold your positions!' cried Bellona.

Felix fired again and Mrs Burden sped down the hill.

'Felix, this is your final warning. Get your sister back in the jar and retreat, now!'

Felix stuck his tongue out at Bellona. 'Leave Livi and the mortals alone then, you big bully-bum!' He flapped his wings, gliding effortlessly towards Romulus and Remus before firing a single laser beam. The chain binding them fizzled and turned to dust, the silver cast slowly fading and releasing the twins from its hold.

Bellona cracked her whip at Felix, narrowly missing his clawed feet. He fired another laser beam and the whip turned to dust, only for the particles to reform, the thong thrashing like a trapped snake as Bellona grabbed hold of the handle.

Felix fired again.

'You can't win, Mother,' cried Romulus. He was still a little off-blue, the snakes droopier than usual, but he seemed OK for a dude who'd been encased in silver. Closely followed by Remus, Tiber and Poly, he squared up to Bellona, standing a few feet in front of her, Scylla rearing to her full height in front of the fort. 'Together, we stand beside the Undecided. Spare the mortals and stand down.'

'Yeah,' said Tiber, 'Sorry, Mamma-Dude, but slaughtering mortals just isn't cool.'

'Naughty, Mama,' said Poly, shaking her fist.

'Oh, I see. Like that, is it? You ungrateful brats!' Bellona looked up at a purple light hovering just below the clouds. She turned towards me and smiled. 'Well, you may have won the battle, but you haven't won the war!'

CHAPTER 35

THE BETRAYAL

What the flamingo tongues?! The hovering purple light was now hurtling towards us, the sky the colour of watery Ribena. Through its blackberry haze emerged a horse-drawn chariot. It thudded to a stop in front of the fort, drenching the LARPers in muddy spray.

'Hi-de-hoot-hoot, everyone!'

No way! Athene Noctua! Only she wasn't Athene Noctua as I knew her. She was in human form. Tall and thin with a beaky nose, her short brown hair was streaked with strands of white, the high collar on her magnificent feathered cloak framing her round face. Her amber eyes were the same, though. And she was just as annoying.

'Well done, chick,' she said. 'I see you put up quite the fight. Shame I had to betray you.'

A tiny bit of sick forced its way up from my stomach. *Tell me this isn't real.*

'Oh, it's real, all right. Not how I'd planned it, but if someone offers you human form, you're going to take it. You do understand, don't you? There's only so much throwing up pellets an owl can take.'

'The mortal!' said Bellona.

'Oh, yes, sorry hon.' Athene Noctua retrieved a carrier-bag sized sack from the bottom of the chariot. Its contents wriggling and squirming, she threw it on to the ground and dabbed. Yes, I know, the dab took me by surprise too. I mean, nobody dabs any more! Not even Dad. But, anyway, back to the sack . . . because it had started to grow, the woven material stretching and distending until it eventually burst and fell away, revealing a crumpled figure dressed in a familiar maroon tunic.

'Dad!' I ran towards him, landing heavily on the sodden grass as Bellona's whip wrapped around my ankles.

Romulus drew his sword. I signalled for him to stop. I couldn't risk Dad getting hurt.

'Wise move,' said Athene Noctua, helping Dad up on to his feet and twisting his arm up his back. 'We'd hate for anything to happen to your precious daddy now, wouldn't we? He's still under the effects of the compression, but he'll be coming round . . . any . . . second . . . NOW!'

Dad shivered, shaking his head like he'd just sucked on a really sour lemon. 'All right, love?' he said. 'I see you've finally met your mother, then. Never did think much of her friends—'

'Another **balatro**!' Athene Noctua tightened her hold on Dad, loosening her grip again as he cried out in pain. 'Oops, sorry, did that hurt? Still getting used to my new form. It would seem my strength is almost as colossal as my wisdomnous!'

'But not as colossal as your ego,' said Dad.

'Silence! I'll have you know, self-love is not the same as conceit—'

Bellona rolled her eyes. 'How about you both put a sock in it! You have done well, Athene Noctua, and you have been rewarded. You don't have to go on about it for the whole of eternity. Now, hand me the mortal!'

Athene Noctua let go of Dad. She raised her hands towards Bellona. 'Chill your chariot, lady!'

Bellona gave Athene Noctua a look that would have turned a mortal to dust. She cracked her whip, wrapping it around Dad's wrist and pulling him towards her. 'And my donkey of a brother and his lava army?' she continued. 'What of them?'

'Vulcs is trapped in the Underworld, as instructed. And it would appear his soldiers are a little low on charge.' Athene Noctua winked, her skin rippling like magma. She twirled around, sparks of energy shooting from her billowing cape. 'Whereas I, after draining their power, have never felt so energized.'

'How could you?' I lunged at Athene Noctua – the electric shock from the energy field around her forcing me back again. 'You said you wanted to help me.'

'Oh, don't be like that, Silvia. You of all people should know how hard it is to pick a side. In the end, you've got to look out for yourself. Have the centuries not taught you mortals anything?'

'It's over, Silvia,' said Bellona. She drew her jewelled dagger. 'Now give me the arrow.'

I looked around for Kenzo. If there was ever a time for my big plan to kick in it was now. But Kenzo had disappeared—

'I said, give me the arrow!' Locking eyes with me, Bellona put the blade of her dagger to Dad's neck.

'Nice to see you too, Bea!' he said. 'You look great!'

'How many times do I have to tell you people to

shut up! Silvia, I'm not playing games here. Hand the arrow over or your father gets it.'

*Ooh, I'll give her the arrow all right. I'll let both those double-crossing **Janus**-faced goddesses have it!*

'Don't even bother,' said Athene Noctua. 'By the time you load your bow, he'll be dead. And so will your little mortal chums.'

Potty-Mouth and the Praetorian Guard! They'd flanked the LARPers, closing in on them from either side of the fort.

I gripped the arrow, my insides molten. *How can I possibly win with Athene Noctua reading my every thought?*

'You can't,' she said. 'Annoying, isn't it?'

'Livi.' Dad's voice was calm and reassuring. 'You know in your heart what you must do.'

'I said quiet!' Bellona's aura flashed scarlet, a wave of searing heat forcing me backwards. I landed on my bum, the arrow flying out of my hand.

'Ooh, thank you very much,' said Athene Noctua as the arrow landed right at her feet. 'Don't mind if I do.' She picked up the arrow and ran her fingers over the crimson fletching.

Bellona held out her hand. 'Hand it over, then.'

'Mmm, not sure as I will.'

'Pardon?'

'My wisdomnous has decided against it.'

'Enough!' cried Bellona, flinging Dad to the floor. He cried out as his forehead slammed against a rock. 'Give me the arrow!'

'Stop it, both of you!' Remus ran towards Dad.

Weapons poised, Tiber and Romulus closed in on Athene Noctua and Bellona, Felix circling above.

'A true god doesn't treat the mortals like this,' said Romulus.

'Oh, back off, worm head.' Athene Noctua shook her cloak, a cloud of feathers forming around her. They hovered in the air, sharpened shafts pointing towards the LARPers. 'Poison. Harvested from your very own snakes while you dreamt. A mortal dies every time you take a step closer.'

'Impressive, Athene Noctua,' said Bellona. 'But you're getting too big for your feathery boots. Now give me the arrow before I wring your scrawny neck.'

'I really don't think so. I've had enough of being bossed around. It's time to rewrite the myths and show the world my wisdomnous. Now, off you go back to Romana. Britannia is mine.'

'Never!' cried Bellona. 'I'll see it crumble first. And every single mortal with it.' She made a grab for her spear and turned towards her legions. '**Cuneum formate**, now!'

CHAPTER 36

THE RETURN OF JUPITER

Behind me, Bellona's front line formed a wedge and closed in on the fort, raising their shields over their mouths to amplify the sound of their deep guttural war cry. Athene Noctua may have dropped her poisonous feathers, but it was out of the **fretale** and into the fire for the LARPers. If help was coming, it better come fast.

'Stand down, both of you!' cried Romulus. 'Bloodshed is not the answer.'

Brow furrowed, he glanced over at Remus, who was taking Dad's pulse. *Why wasn't he moving?* Still winded from my fall, I forced myself on to my feet. Bellona's soldiers were just metres away.

But just as I was wondering if anyone would come to my funeral, the soldiers paused. Their fierce cries replaced by a low droning buzz, they stared up at the gunmetal sky.

Out the corner of my eye, I saw Remus helping Dad to his feet.

'What now?' said Bellona. 'This place is like the Circus Maximus for comings and goings.'

The buzzing grew louder.

Bellona's front line buckled, frenzied soldiers stumbling backwards, eyes still fixed on the sky.

'Silvia?' Hands on hips, Athene Noctua studied the hundreds of silver drones descending on the valley. 'I knew you were up to something, you little minx.'

Sure she did. But she didn't know what. For once I'd kept my thoughts to myself. She wasn't going to see my next move coming either. Channelling my inner Poly, I ran at Athene Noctua full pelt, headbutting her in the stomach. She flew backwards, crashing into her chariot and dropping the arrow. I made a grab for it.

'Seize her!' cried Bellona.

Potty-Mouth jumped down from the fort, followed by his henchmen. He smiled, teeth almost blinding me, and pointed his sword at my chest.

Tiber charged towards him swinging a mace. 'Don't think so, dude!'

The drones were right above us now, multi-coloured strobes shining bright against the stormy sky.

Somewhere in the distance, I heard an engine roar.

Music wavered on the breeze.

'**Recedete!**' called a booming voice. *Retreat!*

Potty-Mouth and his goons edged backwards.

The voice again. 'Retreat, Romana, or feel my wrath!'

Horses whinnied nervously and legionaries fell to their knees as the drones swarmed above the fort, where they formed the shape of a giant angry Jupiter. They hung there for a moment before starting to pulse, the sky awash with rainbow lightning as Jupiter began to dance. Which was definitely not in the script, but like I was going to complain when Kenzo had managed to get his mates in the Harry Styles special effects team to put on a drone show especially for Bellona's legions. A drone show that was scaring the stuffed dormice out of them – just as I'd hoped.

'I said, retreat!' Soldiers scattered as a silver truck with a loudhailer on top tore towards us. 'By order of Jupiter.'

The laser beams were going ballistic now, the sky ablaze with the wildest, most colourful lightning storm ever as the dancing Jupiter strutted his stuff, Harry-style! Potty-Mouth threw himself to the ground, swearing allegiance to the king of gods, his whole body shaking.

Skidding in the mud, the truck slowed in front of the fort. 'I said, retreat! On your feet and do one!' *Kenzo!* Judging by the huge grin, he was enjoying himself a little too much. The loudhailer crackling, he turned up the music, a flurry of drones separating and descending on Bellona's armies in a frenzy of laser-induced lightning!

Frantic legionaries pushed and shoved each other out of the way, fighting to escape the wrath of the dancing Jupiter. Chanting the lyrics to 'Golden', the LARPers legged it after them, waving their weapons in time to the music as they raced past me and chased them down the hill. So much for the grunge infatuation! It was total Harry carnage.

I'd done it. I'd found another way. A way to decide this, without bloodshed. And people had trusted me enough to make it happen. Even Harry Styles's crew! Who I must say were doing a banging job. The dancing Jupiter exploded in a frenzy of thunderbolts as the drones lifted up into the sky again, spelling out the slogan '**Clementiam omnibus**'. Nice – the Latin equivalent of *treat people with kindness*. I looked over to the truck to give Kenzo the thumbs up, but he'd abandoned it, engine still running, the driver's door wide open.

And then I saw why.

Gripping a bronze spear, he was legging it after Bellona.

She was in her chariot. And there, tied to a ruby-embossed sledge being pulled along behind her, was Dad.

Swerving to avoid a frenzied horse that had thrown its rider, I made my way down the slope. 'Stop!' I called. 'Stop!'

Bellona continued to weave her way through the fleeing soldiers, beating them out of the way with her trumpet, Kenzo chasing after her, spear poised.

'Stop!' Didn't he realize it was useless, even if he could get a clean shot. 'STOP!'

Kenzo turned around to look at me, but Bellona continued forward. Reaching the gravel access road, she picked up speed.

'Please! You're going to kill him.'

Bellona pulled the chariot to a sudden stop, the horses rearing. She turned towards me. 'That's kind of the idea.'

Spear raised, Kenzo raced towards the chariot.

'Back off, mortal!' Bellona threw her trumpet, knocking Kenzo out cold. 'Keep your little friends under control, Silvia. Next time it will be my sword.'

Kenzo groaned, which I took as a good sign. I reached for the arrow. 'Let my dad go!'

'Yes,' said Dad, fighting against his restraints. 'Untie me. Sledging just isn't the same without snow.'

'Fine,' said Bellona. 'I'll be right on it. Just as soon as I get enough height to smash your skull.'

'Now, I know you don't mean that, Bea,' said Dad. 'What happened to me being your Adonis and all that?'

'You always had a smart mouth, Ben. I'll admit, I used to find it endearing. But it's time to shut you up once and for all.' Bellona cracked her knuckles, her cape billowing dramatically. 'Unless, that is, Silvia, you'd like to reconsider. I can protect you. You and your precious daddy here.'

'I don't need your protection.'

'I think you do. Especially now Athene Noctua has had a whiff of power. I let her go while I dealt with more pertinent issues, but she'll be back. Now fetch me my trumpet and climb aboard.'

'Never!' I loaded the arrow.

'I can offer you immortality, Silvia. A life fit for the goddess you are destined to become. All you have to do is give me that arrow.'

Immortality. Vulcan had mentioned something about that too. It would be kind of handy, I suppose. Nobody would pick on me on the school bus—

'Tempting, isn't it?'

Not really. Not given the cost. 'Actually, I can't think of anything worse than spending eternity with you!'

Bellona held her arms out to the side. 'Let me

make it easy for you, then. Go on – shoot.'

Blood thundered in my ears as time stood still.

'Didn't think so. Athene Noctua saw it in your dreams – you didn't even have the bottle to finish off a fly! It's embarrassing, really. My own daughter.'

Embarrassing! She'd just threatened to kill everyone between here and Hexham and I was the one who was embarrassing.

'Let my dad go!'

'Well, I guess this is goodbye, then. Would love to hang around, but I've got an empire to build.' Bellona lashed her whip around her trumpet and pulled it back towards her. 'You know how it is. People to see, people to slay. Talking of which, expect a daddy delivery any second. May as well start as I intend to go on with the tyranny.'

I raised the bow. I had to end this for all our sakes. Bellona wasn't lying. She wouldn't be happy until she'd taken the world.

But . . .

. . . she . . .

. . . was my mother.

'One potato.' Dad's voice was kind and nurturing. The exact opposite of Bellona. 'Come on, Livi. From the start. You know the drill.'

We repeated the words together.

'One potato!'

Dad was right. I could do this.

'Two potato.'

I had to do this.

'Three potato.

'Fire!'

CHAPTER 37

WIND AND WEE

Darkness fell and a furious wind tore through the valley. It tugged at my hair and tunic, almost knocking me sideways. Soldiers and LARPers fell to their knees as the darkness turned to light, clouds pulsating with streaks of gold and purple.

It was done.

Finally, the wind grew still.

The only sound was that of a baby's high-pitched cry.

After checking on Dad, who was surprisingly upbeat for a man who'd literally just been dragged through a hedge backwards, I climbed into Bellona's chariot, where a screaming newborn lay on a turquoise velvet cape, her plump cheeks as red and angry as Vulcan's furnace.

I picked the baby up. It kicked furiously and weed on my tunic. Yep, it was Bellona all right.

CHAPTER 38

BEST DAY EVER

A perfect hit!

The arrow glanced off the brass door knocker and landed next door in Mrs Burden's hollyhocks. Smiling, I opened my bedroom window and waved, grateful that some things never change.

'Hurry up, then!' Dad grinned, his centurion

cape flapping in the wind. 'They're here.'

Adjusting my ceremonial tunic, I grabbed my cape and thundered down the stairs. Arm in arm with Dad, I made my way across the drive to the paddock, where Kenzo was greeting the guests with Mina and Jackson, who it turns out hadn't been avoiding me at all. They really were just busy with dance rehearsals and the school play. They waved, faces pink with excitement, before going back to handing out centurion helmets to anyone not in costume. Behind them, Hadrian's Wall cut the sparse landscape in two, the late-afternoon sun casting a golden glow over its ancient stones. Dad was right. This really was the best place for a celebration party.

Honestly, it was going to be brill. Better than brill! A mini LARP in our own back garden. Only today there'd be no hitting each other with latex weapons – we'd had enough of fighting. Today was all about celebrating. Celebrating our differences and what brought us together.

'So, Livi,' Dad's dark, shoulder-length hair

danced in the breeze, 'are you ready to party?'

'I very much hope so, sister,' said a familiar voice.

His snake hair bobbing to the beat of the music, Romulus emerged from behind Mrs Burden's toga-clad bingo group, who were gathered around Harry Styles, checking out his new Chanel handbag. Yes. Harry. Styles. At. Our. House. He'd got chatting to Mrs Burden at the local Londis. Apparently, he'd been really annoyed his security team wouldn't let him come along and join the battle against Bellona in person!

Anyway, enough about Harry. This is my story. And I was about to power hug my gorgon brother!

'I've been practising my dance moves!' he said, hugging me tight before taking my hand and spinning me round on the rough plywood dance floor. 'I'm looking forward to shaking my snakes to some more of this Harry pop music.' He twirled, falling over his own feet.

Erg, OK. This was going to be interesting, but so long as Romulus was having fun that was all that mattered. I mean, brilliant or what! All my brothers and sisters here in Once Brewed, ready to party. Turns out LARP was the perfect way to explain your unusual extended family, and with everyone in fancy dress they'd fit in just fine. Even Scylla was here. She had a new blingy pram Dad had made using a fish tank and the frame off an old baby buggy.

'Mama!'

'Poly!' I lifted up my mini cyclops sister and she planted a slobbery kiss on my nose.

'Mama, hug!' she said.

Remus came in for a hug next. I threw my arms around him and squealed, Tiber playfully nudging Remus out of the way and wrapping his arms around me, careful not to squash baby Bellona, who was in a sling strapped to his chest. Even she seemed to be in a good mood, despite smelling a bit whiffy.

'Not again!' said Tiber, holding his nose and trotting off to change her nappy.

Laughing, I took hold of Poly's hand and looked around the paddock. Dad and the LARPers had done a brilliant job building the stage and dance floor. Like the food stands, they were decorated with brightly coloured bunting and balloons, fairy lights strung loosely around their wooden frames. Hot dogs. Candy floss. Pink lemonade. This was going to be the best day ever.

But then I saw him.

Rory Smartwart.

Lurking by the lemonade stand with his dad.

He stared at me, open-mouthed, gripping his cardboard cup so tightly it dinted, pink lemonade sloshing over the top. My stomach lurched like Bellona's chariot. I'd managed to avoid him in school recently. But there was no avoiding him now. Or his dad.

'What you looking at, son?' Mr Smartwart's brow furrowed. Scratching his chin, he looked from me to Poly, eyes scrunched like he was struggling to believe what he was seeing. Here we go again . . .

Dweebs.

Weirdos.

Losers.

I knew what he was thinking. What most people think.

But they were wrong. My family may be a little unconventional, but we were not dweebs or losers. *Weird?* OK, I'll give them that, but who wants to be normal anyway? Waving at Chitra and the twins, who were handing out replica centurion helmets to my maths teacher and her children, I took a deep breath and led Poly over to Mr Smartwart.

'Hello, Mr Smartwart,' I said. 'Hello, Rory.'

'Oh, hiya, pet.' Mr Smartwart rubbed his eyes. 'Sorry, I cannet see a thing without me glasses. Second pair to go missing this month. Lost the first pair when I was doing the Burdens' windows the other week. Don't suppose you've seen them, have you?'

'No, sorry, Mr Smartwart.'

'Call me Mike, please.' Smiling, he looked around the paddock. 'Canny set up you have here. Smashing costumes.'

'Mama!'

Mr Smartwart – I mean Mike – smiled warmly at the snotty-nosed cyclops.

'This is my sister, Poly.'

'Mama,' agreed Poly.

'Pleased to meet you too,' laughed Mike. 'What a cutie, hey Rory?'

'Yes,' agreed Rory, licking lemonade off his fingers. He had a latex mask sticking out of his back pocket. Was that an attempt at fancy dress?

'How's it going, dude?' Tiber said, trotting over to join us with baby Bellona. 'I'm Tiber. Psyched to meet you.'

'And I'm Romulus. Silvia's brother and loyal servant to Romana.'

'Pleased to meet you,' said Mr Smartwart. 'Amazing make-up. Do you work in television too?'

'Actually, I'm hoping to be in Harry's next video,' said Romulus, looking over enviously at the bingo group. 'I've been practising my dance moves especially.'

Well, you couldn't knock his ambition, and the last few weeks had proved anything was possible. I left them chatting about Harry Styles's jumpsuit collection – what can I say, Romulus was obsessed – and made my way to the far corner of the paddock, waving hello to Felix and Uncle Vulcan, who had been put in charge of the hog roast and were taking their responsibilities very seriously. Almost as seriously as Mr Burden, who was on the pudding stand and wasn't letting a broken arm get in the way of a good cake batter. Him and Uncle Vulcan were besties these days – their friendship fuelled by a love of all things sweet.

He visited us most days now, Uncle Vulcan, often sleeping over on the settee so he could watch old movies and eat junk food. Dad had had to order an extra recycling bin for all his pop bottles. As for the sweet wrappers he left all over the place, let's not go there. Let's just say that *mostly* it was brilliant having him around, even if he did go on continuously about how much he hated the dark of the Underworld.

Yeah, you're right, I was so lucky to have all these people around me. The LARPers too – people who'd stood by us when things got really tough; who didn't care about our differences; who just wanted to do the right thing. My family was bigger than I had ever realized.

But it was Dad I wanted to find right now. My lovely dad who had loved me from day one and never put any conditions on it. My special dad who had welcomed my strange new family with all his heart. And who had hardly batted an eyelid when I'd shot my own mother with a sacred arrow and she'd turned into a baby. I needed to tell him how grateful I was. How much he meant to me.

CHAPTER 39

ENOUGH

Running the last few steps across the bustling paddock, I made my way to the bell tent. Tiber said Dad had gone there to make sure everything was set up for the big sleepover. There wasn't enough room for everyone in the house, so we were making camp Romana-style.

'Dad?'

I pulled back the tent flap.

'Dad!'

'Can you see yer father?' spat Mrs Burden. She was stacking a fancy china cake stand with **ambrosia** cake. The gold leaf glistened in the low light of the oil burners.

I shook my head.

'No! Didn't think so. Now shush, I'm concentrating.'

'But Tiber said he was in here.'

'*But Tiber said he was in here*,' Mrs Burden mimicked.

Yep, she was just as charming as ever. Some things never change, I guess.

'Sent him with Kevin to fetch me **vasa diatreta**. What was the man thinking? Who drinks nectar out of paper cups?'

Dad had drawn a line at the flamingo tongues and dormice Mrs Burden wanted to cook – some things were better left in Romana! – but he had agreed to the ambrosia and nectar. After all, as Mrs Burden had insisted, you can't invite a bunch of gods round for a knees-up and expect them to drink tea.

'What you gawking at?' Mrs Burden straightened the lace doily she'd placed under the jug of nectar to soak up the condensation.

'Nothing.'

Though I suppose I had been gawking a bit. Questioning. Wondering. What it would be like to drink the golden liquid. Vulcan had said it was true – that I really could choose immortality and spend eternity with my brothers and sisters. He also said it was a decision not to be taken lightly.

'Livi! There you are.'

Dad. Seriously, he was so happy he was glowing like a god. His dream had come true. While Rome Play hadn't exactly gone to plan, it had brought people together. Proved we didn't have to be like everyone else to be accepted. I put my arms around him and hugged him tight.

'Thank you,' I said.

'For what?'

'For being you.'

Dad smiled. 'How could I be anything else?'

And I knew exactly what he meant. Maybe one day I'd feel differently about drinking the nectar. But for now, this was enough. It was time to go and dance to Harry Styles.

Erg, make that dance *with* Harry Styles! He was already strutting his stuff on the dance floor when we went back outside. Mrs Burden's bingo group had made a circle around him. They clapped their hands and cheered, taking it in turns to move into the centre of the circle and copy Harry's moves.

'I'm back,' cried Romulus, weaving his way through the dancers and linking Harry. 'Must say, I am really enjoying your portable latrinas. Now, will you show me how to do that groovy hip swing again?'

'Do you think we should rescue him?' Dad smiled, nodding towards Harry.

There was a shout from the DJ stand. 'Let's mix this up!' cried Kenzo. Nirvana's 'Smells Like Teen Spirit' blared from the speakers.

Mrs Burden's bingo group let out a collective groan but then Harry began to pogo. He shook his hair, grunge-style. Romulus and the bingo group joined in. And the LARPers. Harry seemed just fine!

'Come on, Livi!' screamed Dad. 'Let's dance!'

'Yo, fam!' Fist-bumping Dad, Tiber made room in the circle next to him and Remus, Felix zooming around us with Scylla's pram as we strutted our stuff with Harry. But there was someone missing.

Standing on my tippy-toes, I looked over towards the barbecue stand. Uncle Vulcan was chatting to Chitra, who was sharing a giant hot dog with the twins.

I fought my way through the partygoers towards them. 'Come on!' I said, taking Chitra's hand. 'On the dance floor! You too, Uncle Vulcan!'

Uncle Vulcan handed the tongs to Mr Burden and followed us into the dance frenzy. He twirled, tunic billowing. He wiggled his shoulders and snapped his fingers – proper dad dancing. At least he was trying, I suppose. And it was so cool to have all my family around me. It made everything that had happened in Romana worth it. Though, I guess, it would have been better if my mum hadn't turned out to be a bloodthirsty tyrant. Oh well, can't have everything. Maybe Baby Bellona would be different!

Ari and Avi joining in with Felix's whizzy pram game, Chitra took Dad's hand and smiled. I smiled too. I had my brothers and sisters. Maybe Dad needed something else as well. I edged away from him. Along with Uncle Vulcan, Remus and Tiber, I joined Romulus and Harry, who were moshing by the stage.

'Great party,' said Harry, his hair bouncing as he jumped up and down in time to the music. 'Nice one!'

Nice one indeed. Everything was golden.

GLOSSARY

Hello, it's me again – Livi!

I know not all of you are mega into Rome and LARP, like me, so I thought I'd explain some of the words and phrases from the book. Not all of them mind – I've not got time for that, what with things kicking off again big-style in Romana – but I'm sure you'll have fun looking up anything I've left out for yourself.

AENEID, THE a seriously long poem by Roman poet Virgil. Tells the story of Aeneas and the founding of Rome.

AMBROSIA a god's favourite scran. In Romana, served as a cake.

ASINE NEBULO Latin for 'donkey trash'. Common insults, not necessarily used together.

AUXILIARY soldier in the Roman army who wasn't a Roman citizen. Paid less and more likely to die, but on the plus side, if they survived their term they were rewarded with citizenship.

BALATRO a bit like a jester. Told bad jokes to rich people at fancy dinner parties. Also found at big events, warming up the crowds.

BASILICA one of the fancy buildings you'll find in the **forum**. A bit like your town hall crossed with the city law courts with some shops thrown in for good measure.

BELLONARI Bellona's priests or cult members. Interesting chaps!

BONA PUELLA Latin for 'good girl'. How patronizing is my mother?!

CALCEUS (PLURAL 'CALCEI') Roman equivalent to a walking boot. Made your feet smelly in warmer parts of the empire so sandals or open boots were preferred there.

CASTRA Roman fortress or camp. Marching camps were seriously epic, with wooden ramparts and defensive ditches, but just imagine having to set all that up every night after walking twenty miles.

CAUTE Latin for 'careful'. As in, *Caute, you're about to become griffin fodder, yer muppet!*

CENTURION thinks he's hard and won't think twice about hitting you with his whacking stick if you step out of line. In charge of a unit of eighty soldiers. Wears a fancy plumed helmet.

CLEMENTIAM OMNIBUS 'Kindness for all'. The Latin equivalent of 'treat people with kindness'. A Harry Styles mantra rather than a Roman one, the Romans being more into pillaging and conquering than being nice.

CONTUBERNIUM a unit of eight soldiers who all slept in the same leather tent. Bet that smelt nice.

COVENTINA the goddess of lamb fries. Only kidding. She's the Celtic goddess of wells and springs, and one of the many local gods adopted by the Romans because they liked to hedge their bets.

CUNEUM FORMATE military manoeuvre where soldiers form a wedge and charge the enemy line – useful when wishing to annihilate your opponent.

DOMUS a Roman home or dwelling – in this case, a proper posh one.

FATES, THE or rather the *parcae*, as they were known in Ancient Rome. The masters of your destiny – old Nona, Decuma and Morta mapped out your life at birth, even deciding when you'd die. Yeah, right.

FORTUNA the goddess of fortune. Depending on her mood, she might bring good or bad luck. Best hope she's in a good mood before your next test.

FORUM the place to be in Ancient Rome if you want to go shopping, hang out with your mates, do business or sacrifice a bull. It's all happening at the forum!

FRESCO Roman wall painting. Paint is applied when the plaster is wet, which makes it part of the wall's surface.

FRETALE Roman frying pan. Useful for sautéing flamingo tongues.

GAMEMASTER the gamemaster is in charge of running a LARP. They often write the game and do a lot of the organizing too. They are supported by the crew.

GAUL the name given by the Romans to the Celtic tribespeople of northern Italy and mainland western Europe, including all of what is now France.

GLADIUS Latin for 'sword' but most commonly used to describe the short sword used by Roman soldiers. Most excellent for stabbing your enemy at close range.

HADRIAN'S WALL very long wall built by the Roman emperor Hadrian across northern Britannia. It runs from what is now Tyne and Wear to Bowness-on-Solway in Western Cumbria, and was built to keep the Caledonian out cos they were harder than the Romans.

HOSPITIUM the divine duty of hospitality. Be nice to your guests or, for that matter, total strangers who just turn up at your door – or feel the wrath of the gods!

IMPLUVIUM a pool usually found in the main room of a Roman house used to catch rainwater off the open sloping roof. Definitely not for weeing in!

INTERVALLUM the space deliberately left between the ramparts and the tents in a Roman marching camp. Don't put your tent up in the intervallum unless you want to be the first to be hit by an incoming missile or like sleeping with the livestock.

JANUS Roman god of doorways and transitions. Had two faces – one looking forward to the future, the other back to the past.

LAMB FRIES you might think you want to know what lamb fries are, but seriously, you don't. Don't say I didn't warn you if you decide to google.

LARP OR LIVE-ACTION ROLE-PLAY a role-playing game where you dress up as your chosen character and act out the game. There are lots of types of LARP, including high fantasy, zombie or alien invasions or, yes, even Ancient Rome. Give it a go. You won't regret it!

LARPE DIEM Dad's sad twist on *carpe diem* – Latin for 'seize the day'. Which basically means enjoy yourself before you snuff it.

LEGIONARY legionaries were soldier dudes known for their red capes and love of marching. Got twenty-five years to spare? Then become a legionary!

MORS the personification of death – you definitely don't want her chasing you while you are in a flying chariot.

NECTAR the gods' favourite liquid refreshment. Drink it with ambrosia cake to top up your godliness.

NEREIDS sea nymphs. The daughters of Nereus, an ancient god sometimes called the old man of the sea.

PERISTYLE a continuous columned porch surrounding a building, garden or courtyard. Also sometimes used to refer to a garden or space surrounded by such columns. Excellent for playing hide and seek!

PISCINA a small pool or pond. Not for lazing around and feasting in!

PLEBEIAN a member of the common people. Just a normal bod, like you and me.

PORTICO a columned walkway or porch you'll find on a lot of Roman buildings. Go up the temple steps through the columns and, hey presto, you are hanging out in the portico.

PRAETORIAN GUARD an elite unit of the Roman army. Think MI5 only with fewer gadgets – they acted as spies and personal bodyguards for the emperor and senior officials.

PUPA Latin for 'doll'. Do not call me 'doll'!

RECEDETE Latin for 'retreat'. As in, your number's up and you'd better get out of here, soldier!

RUDIS wooden training sword.

SAGITTARII Roman archers. Usually non-citizens, as true Romans like their combat up-close and personal. It's more manly to fight with a sword, apparently. Seriously, these dudes!

SALVE Latin for 'hail' or 'hello'. Like, *Salve rich person, let's go and eat some flamingo tongues.*

SENATE HOUSE (CURIA) the senate house is where the senate met, which is not much help if you don't know what the senate is. You really should have listened in school.

SIBYL prophetess or oracle who could help predict your future and/or help you have a chat with the gods about their divine will. Prima sibyl – the first Romanan sibyl.

SILPHIUM also known as laserwort, which is a weird name for a herb right? Anyway, the Romans loved it and used it to flavour food, cure ailments, and as a perfume.

SUBSISTO Latin for 'stop' or 'desist'! Obvious, really!

TABERNAE that's shops to you and me. Often found on the front of fancy town houses to protect their residents from crime and the noise of the street.

TALI Roman dice-type game usually played with sheep or goat knucklebones. Many a legionary has lost his weekly wage playing tali.

TERSORIUM a stick with a sponge stuck to the end used to wipe your bum. The Romans didn't mind sharing them either – cleaning the sponge with salt water or vinegar solution.

VASA DIATRETA posh Roman glass goblets, which Mrs Burden never stops going on about. They have a carved decorative cage surrounding the inner glass beaker and are right fancy.

ACKNOWLEDGEMENTS

My first thank you must go to my godly editor Ronnie-Rachel Leyshon and divine agent Kate Shaw. Thank you for sticking with me during a turbulent time and believing my words were worth waiting for. Ronnie, this book is as much yours as mine. I hate that you are always right – well *almost* always.

Writing a book is a team effort and thanks also must go to Barry Cunningham and the wider Chicken House team: Rachel Hickman, Kesia Lupo, Laura Myers, Elinor Bagenal, Jazz Bartlett Love, Liv Jeggo, Laura Smythe and Emily Groom-Collis. Could there be a better team to have behind me? Erg no! Thanks also to copy-editor Fraser Crichton, proofreader Esther Waller and Latin guru Nicholas Bowling.

And if a book really is only as good as its cover, I am truly blessed to have my cover illustrated by real-life Roman Flavia Sorrentino. Flavia, thank you so much. I could not adore this cover and the chapter headers any more if I had been hit by Cupid's arrow. Thanks also to cover designer Steve Wells – it looks amazing!

Thank you to my Adonis-kebab, Mark, for always being there and never doubting I'd find my way out of the depths of the Underworld. And thanks to the mighty Titan Dylan for keeping it real – I'll *silly goose, <u>you</u>*!

A huge thank you also to the divine writing friends who have supported me over the last few years: the Swaggers, Foresters, Juvenile Litters, SCBWIers and all the authors and illustrators I've been lucky enough to befriend on my writing journey. Particular thanks to Lou Cliffe-Minns, Catherine Whitmore and Anna Mainwaring for the lockdown walks and book chat and to Danielle Jawando for the author/lecturer camaraderie. A big thank you also to Louie Stowell for an amazing cover reveal and being a brilliant support to the writing community. People say writing is a lonely business, but that's not been my experience. The children's book community is an amazing thing to be part of and I am so grateful to everyone who has advised, supported and championed me.

Key to that community, of course, are the wonderful bloggers, librarians, booksellers, festival staff, teachers and literacy advocates who work so hard to encourage reading for pleasure and get our books into the hands of readers. You deserve your own temple on the Palatine Hill, and I raise a glass of nectar to you all.

And, of course, thanks also to all the friends and family, who have continued to cheer me on from the sidelines, especially Mum and Dad to whom this book is dedicated. A big thank you to the BMX community for embracing *Princess BMX* and to the LARPers who inspired this latest book. Special thanks also to Indy and Evie for being my junior children and young people consultants and stopping me sounding too much like an old person. Thanks also to Hannah for advising me on my North-East accent and to LARP beta readers Cam, Charlie, Jules and Merri.

And, finally, thanks to everyone who has read

one of my books. Meeting young readers at events and school visits is one of the best parts of the job and I salute you all!

PRINCESS BMX

Trust me, the fairy tales have it so wrong. Dingy towers and wicked stepmums are the least of my worries: it's the boredom that will kill me. Honestly, apart from the endless supply of cupcakes, being a princess is pretty rubbish. I used to think about locking myself in a tower and throwing away the key. Thank the good goblin I discovered BMX. If it wasn't for BMX, nothing would have changed . . .

> '. . . a daft and delicious fantasy.'
> THE GUARDIAN

perback, ISBN 978-1-911490-94-4, £6.99 • ebook, ISBN 978-1-912626-42-7, £6.99